Lucid

By Natalie Roers

Twilight Times Books
Kingsport Tennessee

Lucid

This is a work of fiction. All concepts, characters and events portrayed in this book are used fictitiously and any resemblance to real people or events is purely coincidental.

Copyright © 2013 Natalie Roers

All rights reserved. No part of this book may be reproduced, stored in a retrieval system or transmitted in any form by any means electronic, mechanical, photocopying, recording or otherwise, except brief extracts for the purpose of review, without the permission of the publisher and copyright owner.

Paladin Timeless Books
Twilight Times Books
P O Box 3340
Kingsport TN 37664
http://twilighttimesbooks.com/

First Edition, July 2013

ISBN: 978-1-60619-027-2

Library of Congress Control Number: 2013911631

Cover art by Ural Akyuz

Book cover design by Heather Bragg

Printed in the United States of America.

*To all my fellow square pegs.
And to Cory and Austin,
who prove every day that my dreams are real.*

Special Thanks to

Lida, Barb, and Leslie. You helped me become a better businesswoman and a stronger writer—for these gifts I am eternally grateful.

Thank you to my parents, my sister, Heather Hoefer-Bragg, Mike Flanagan, Lorraine (Rainy) Boozer-Simpson, Shamos Fisher, Wendy Womack, and Paul—for their friendship, constant words of encouragement, and advice.

Thank you to my son, Austin, for reintroducing me to imagination.

Most of all thank you to my husband, Cory Eglseder, for reading every page and every revision a hundred times over and for all of your brilliant suggestions. You believe I can do anything, but fail to realize you are the reason why.

Chapter 1

Some kids have normal first memories. Maybe they remember a carnival, or the first day of kindergarten, or riding on top of someone's shoulders at a Fourth of July parade.

My first memories are white: white coats, white walls, and white rooms.

But something seems off now as I try to navigate through the once familiar halls of the hospital from my youth. I need to get to room 403, that's my room, but every time I turn a corner it seems I've gotten mixed up somehow and am going the wrong way. I look at the doors for direction, but the numbers on them don't seem to be in any particular order or are missing altogether.

A pretty blonde nurse walks by and I try to stop her to ask for help, but she doesn't seem to notice me. She just keeps looking straight ahead as she walks quickly down the corridor. She carries a clipboard in front of her, obviously planning to attend to more pressing matters. That's when I hear the crying. It stops me in my tracks and raises the hair on the back of my neck. It's a child's voice, that I can tell, and although the sound is faint, something about it is eerily familiar. I turn around, my footsteps echoing down the hallway, and follow the cries to the last room on the right. The lights flicker as I approach the open doorway.

As I poke my head inside, I am surprised to see my mother standing there. She is noticeably younger and even more beautiful than I remember; she has long, wavy, thick dark hair and her bright red lipstick pops against her perfect ivory skin. She's talking very seriously with a stout older man who's wearing thick rimmed spectacles and a stethoscope around his neck. "So it can all be fixed?" she asks.

"Well, not a hundred percent," the man replies. "Because of the macroencephaly, his head circumference will always be a little larger than most, but he'll grow into that more as a man and it won't be as noticeable. Now, as far as the torticollis? Travis *will* most likely retain a fair amount of asymmetry in his face and shoulders, however with the right treatment plan we should be able to make him look and feel a heck of a lot better."

My mother smiles and nods at the doctor.

I remember this conversation, I think.

As they turn toward the examination table, their bodies part, and I am able see myself as I was at three years old. My face and shoulders are grossly misshapen and my head looks like an orange atop a toothpick. My hair is just as dark, curly, and frizzy as it is now, but my skin is smooth and free of acne. I'm sitting on the metal table, my legs dangling in the air, and my face is puffy and red from crying.

They doctor bends down to pat me on the head. "You've seen Gumby, right Travis?"

I look up at him and shake my head yes, my eyes brimming with tears.

"Well, we're gonna stretch you for a while. Kinda like Gumby stretches. Is that all right with you, young man?"

My mother reaches out and grabs my hand. She squeezes it so hard that even as a young child, I know her squeezing my hand is more for her comfort—not the other way around.

The pretty nurse that ignored me earlier now comes up beside me in the hallway and knocks on the door frame.

"Doctor Rosenthal? Here are the charts you asked for." The nurse hands him the files and then looks over at the childhood version of myself. "Aren't you the cutest little guy?" she coos. "Do you want a sucker?" She digs a lollipop out of her pocket.

"Is it okay, Mom?" the nurse asks.

"That's very nice of you, thank you. What do you say, Travis?"

"Thank you," my childhood-self answers shyly.

The nurse smiles politely at everyone and then leaves the room. She still doesn't seem to notice me as she flattens herself against the wall.

Another woman is walking down the hallway towards us and I watch curiously as the nurse motions frantically for the woman to look in the room. The woman appears startled as she pauses in front of the open doorway.

"Come here!" the pretty blonde nurse calls out to her in a hushed tone.

They move a little further down the wall, but I can still hear them as they whisper.

"Yikes, that's a different lookin' kid," the new woman says.

"I know! He's so ugly he's almost cute, isn't he?"

"Cute is the last word I'd use to describe him."

"Did you see who his mother was?" the nurse asks in a gossipy way.

The other woman tries to move past me to look back in, but her friend pulls her back. "Don't do that! They'll see you!"

"Well, who is it?"

"That's Gary Hunter's wife."

"No!" The woman gasps. "The high school football star?"

"Yup, the quarterback and the prom queen's kid."

"Wow, who'd a thought it? Boy, they must be disappointed, huh?" The two women giggle.

I get up off the wall and shout at them as they start walking away.

They can't hear me so they continue laughing as they move down the corridor. Each giggle that trails behind them hits me like shrapnel. *We live in Middle of Nowhere, Indiana. Who do they think they are? Supermodels?*

Smacking the palm of my hand angrily against the wall, I take off running down the hall.

When I get to the end of the hallway, I use my foot to kick open the swinging double doors, but as I do, I find I'm now entering the hallway outside of the biology lab at my high school.

I look around, confused. *Am I late for class? Wait? What class am I supposed to be in, anyway?* The fog of not knowing makes me feel anxious and upset, but I'm not sure how to figure it out so I just try to blend in.

Kids are pouring out of the classrooms, likes ants out of a mound. I envy that they all instinctually seem to know where to go, who to talk to, and how to talk to them.

Just like at the hospital, no one seems to notice me. However, in this place, this doesn't strike me as odd as I've learned how not to draw attention to myself. You'd never know it from my silence in the stands at the pep rallies, but on the inside I'm on my feet hollering and cheering along with the rest of the school.

As everyone rushes past me, I stop to look at a poster of a snarling opossum on the wall. It has a caption that reads, "The Awesome Opossums of Wesley High." The opossum is our mascot, and there are posters just like this one plastered all over the school, but for some reason I can't stop staring at it. Something's not quite right about all of this. There's something that I want to remember, but my mind can't seem to focus.

What is it? What isn't right here?

The more I try to figure it out, the more kids fill the hallway. They start bumping into me, knocking me off balance, but I keep my ground, my eyes fixed on the poster.

"Hey, Hunchback, move!" I hear someone scream. "You're in the way!"

Pep rallies, school, class—what's not right?

The crowd gets thicker and thicker until everyone is standing shoulder to shoulder; packed in like sardines. They all move with the exact same rhythm and I can feel myself starting to being carried off down the hall with the crowd. I look back over my shoulder at the opossum one more time, and as I do, it hits me.

School's out!

"It's out!" I scream at the realization. "School's out!"

None of the blurry, nameless, faces react at all to what I've said, but I'm thrilled with myself for remembering.

"School's out!" I scream again. "You don't have to be here!"

The students keep mindlessly moving down the hallway and I find myself getting angry at their ambivalence.

This is my shining moment and they're ruining it! I think. For me, the summer just means I get to sleep in late. But it's the last summer before our senior year; for everyone else my age, school being out means lazy days at the lake and long nights out, doing things that their parents would kill them for—that is, if their parents ever found out about it.

Here I am, sharing the single greatest piece of news they could ever hear, yet everyone's acting like I'm screaming out the lunch menu!

Disgusted, I use my elbows and shoulders to push through the crowd. A few people I don't recognize give me nasty looks or mutter things under their breath as I move past them, but again, nobody reacts at all to my great revelation that school has ended for the year.

When I get to the stairwell, I stop. Indignant, I look back at the crowd and yell, "Well, I don't know about you, but I don't have to be here, so I'm going home!"

But when I turn back around, instead of seeing the stairs, I see a beautiful pool of crystal clear water. I look behind me and the school is gone. I'm on a diving board suspended high up in the air with nothing around me but blue sky. Normally, I'm afraid of heights, but it doesn't even cross my mind now.

Arching my back, I reach my arms way out to the side and without a second's worth of hesitation let my body fall forward. Air whooshes past my face. For a brief moment I feel the sweet, weightless freedom of falling. This only lasts for a moment, though, before my natural senses suddenly come rushing back.

My stomach flutters. I am completely overcome with the very realistic sensation of tumbling through the air like a skydiver without a parachute. I can feel myself start to panic, and in a desperate attempt to slow the descent start frantically spinning my arms and legs around like pinwheels. I open my mouth to scream. Then just as I am about to hit the water with unthinkable force, my body jerks awake.

It takes me a moment to make the connection, but as I do, I let out a deep sigh of relief. Comforting myself in the same way countless numbers of dreamers have done when things go bump in the night, I tell myself, "It was just a dream."

It was just a dream.

It was just a dream.

I have absolutely no way of knowing that this is the last time I'll ever be able to tell myself that.

I think back on that dream a lot now. It's funny, with everything that happened after, you wouldn't think that this dream would stand

out that much, but it does. That memory represents simpler times…
and that's what we all get nostalgic for, isn't it? Simpler times.

Chapter 2

"I need some pills."

"Ya do, do ya now?" Doctor Kelly chuckled and glanced momentarily up from her desk. She was leafing through a folder of what I only could assume contained my vast and sordid medical history.

"Well, if it isn't my good friend, Travis Hunter. It's good to see you again Trav; it's been awhile." Doctor Kelly smiled. She slapped her hands playfully on her thighs and rolled back on her chair, "walking" a few steps towards me while still seated. "Den I should let you know somezing." She looked around as if others might be listening in.

"Yeah?"

She cupped one hand around the side of her mouth, and in an exaggerated whisper said, "I'm a zerapist. Not a drug dealer."

I smiled from the doorway.

"Now come on in here and sit down. I want to catch up on everyzing dat's been going on wid you."

Kelly's accent wasn't overwhelming, but was definitely detectable. I'd never asked her what it was, maybe German? The only words you could really hear it on were the ones that had a "th" in them. For her it came out sounding more like a "d" or a "z."

She stood up, gave me a warm hug, and patted the chair directly in front of her desk for me to sit down. "Where's your Mom?"

"She had stuff to do at the store."

I watched Doctor Kelly's skirt swish about her legs as she pulled her chair back behind her desk and sat down. She always wore long skirts and soft cotton tops that seemed to float about her when she moved. Kelly was very pretty in an earthy kind of way. She was tall and slender and her long hair was so blonde it looked almost white. I guessed she was probably around forty, but she looked exceptionally good for her age. She didn't have any wrinkles yet. In fact, about the only line on her face was that of an old, thin circular scar that hooked around the outside of her right eye.

"So what's up? How are your folks?" Kelly asked.

"Good, I guess."

"You're about to start da big senior year, aren't you?"

"Yeah."

"I ran into your Dad da odder day. He told me all about da new room dey gave you. Dat's a big deal! You know how many teenagers would kill for somezing like dat?"

I'm not good with small talk. Kelly knows this, but I think it's her way of getting me to practice. Silence is my best defense when I realize I've been taken in. It works well in a number of ways. Mainly, I don't have to answer the questions, but it also it eats up a lot of time so I can stay in her office longer.

"Travis? Your room? Dat's a big deal, huh?"

I took in all the strange statues and prints around her office. It's cool and dark in the room and there's always a faint smell of eucalyptus oil in the air. I liked that.

"Travis? What's going on? You said you wanted some pills when you came in here. What was dat about?"

"Yeah, I can't sleep."

"Dere he is. Welcome back. You can't sleep. Okay, so how long's dis been going on?"

"I'm not sure, a few weeks I guess? Maybe a month or so."

Kelly looked down and scribbled thoughtfully on a piece of paper from the folder.

"So, since about da time school was getting ready to let out. Has anyzing else changed in dat time?"

"Other than me not sleeping?"

"Travis,"

"I dunno." I said, blowing air out of the side of my mouth. "I guess I've had some kinda weird dreams and stuff, too."

Kelly stopped writing and looked up.

"What kind of weird dreams?"

"Just weird school stuff …and, like… I dunno, I guess I'm remembering a lot more of them."

"Huh." Kelly looked momentarily intrigued. When I said nothing more, she shook her head and looked back down.

"Well, we usually treat dat with some kind behavior modification first."

She began digging into a pile of papers on her desk. "I have a handout somewhere in dis mess. You'd be surprised at how a couple of simple changes can really just make a world of difference."

"No."

At first it barely came out as more than a whisper.

"Okay, well I can't seem to find it, but I have a pretty good memory and I can probably-"

"NO!"

The word came out with such force that Kelly flinched—freezing mid-dig.

Everything stood still as our eyes met in the uncomfortable space my outburst had created. Oddly enough, I was the first to break it.

"That was weird. I'm sorry Doctor Kelly. It's just, I don't want a handout. Thank you very much, though. What I'd really like would be to try some sleeping pills." Then almost as an afterthought, like politeness would help my cause, "Please."

Doctor Kelly planted her arms firmly in front of her and instinctively leaned in.

"Now, Travis, you know I'm not da kind of doctor who just gives out pills."

"But you are a real doctor, right? You could if you wanted to."

The jab obviously got under her skin. "I don't believe a real doctor should simply medicate problems," she said. "I believe dey should get to da root of dem, but if you mean do I have a degree? Den, yes, I have several. I'd be happy to show dem to you if you'd like."

I crossed my arms and sulked in retaliation.

It was another failure in my life. The line for the mid-day medication break in my school was just as long as the lunch line. Of course my Mom would've had to set me up with the only psychiatrist across three states that didn't believe in medicating her patients. Unless you counted herbal remedies. Doctor Kelly was a holistic therapist.

Her voice softened. "Travis, why do you zink you need medication?"

"I told you. I have a sleeping problem." Then under my breath I added, "Everyone else does it. I don't know why I can't."

Again silence. My eyes dropped from hers to the floor and then floated back up to settle on the bookcase just over her right shoulder. She watched me closely, waiting for me to say more.

On the shelf in a thick silver frame was a photograph of a man with two small children.

"That's a nice picture," I said. I got up from my seat and walked over to the bookcase.

Doctor Kelly shifted uncomfortably in her seat, absentmindedly brushing her fingers over the scar on the side of her face. "Dank you."

I picked up the photo and looked back at her. "Is this your family?"

She nodded.

"They look good." I said. "They all have nice smiles." My hand lifted self-consciously to my own mangled mouth as I said this, then jerked back down.

Doctor Kelly picked up her pen and tapped the bottom of it on the desk a few times, her face tightening.

I held my breath, waiting for her to take the bait.

It's not like I felt sorry for myself. You see all people use their looks to their advantage. Whereas a beautiful woman might use her sexuality to manipulate people in certain situations, a person with unappealing looks can just as easily use guilt and sympathy to get what they want. It's a basic survival technique.

Even the great Doctor Kelly Jansen was not immune to this strategy. With her many degrees and years of practice she may have had a better idea of what I was doing, but in the end she was still human. She had the basic primal need to help me. "You know," she said, "you're right, Travis. You aren't like everyone else."

Kelly exhaled deeply and stood up. She walked over to me and gently removed the photograph from my hands. After running her hand over the image, Kelly placed the picture back on the shelf. She turned to face me. "I know dat you don't understand dis now, but it's not always a bad zing to be different. It's da people dat go against da grain dat are da most interesting."

"Hm," I hummed. "That's easy for someone like you to say."

"Why?"

"You've never had to deal with not fitting in."

"And how do you know dat?"

"I can just tell," I said, turning away. Leaning over, I began to inspect some of the others items on the shelf.

"Is dat what you want, to fit in?"

"I don't know." I shrugged. "It'd be nice to try, I guess." Then I picked up a little white statue. "What's this?"

"Ahhh," Doctor Kelly sighed. "Dat's Dub-belt-je'."

"Doo-bah-what?"

She laughed. "Dub-belt-je'," Kelly repeated. "According to Dutch folklore Dub-belt-je' was a cat dat saved da life of a beautiful little girl when her grandmodder didn't want her."

"Why didn't her grandmother want her?"

"Because she was a girl."

"Huh." I turned the statue over in my hands. It was made out of stone and had the head of a panther with the body of a man.

"It was a very long time ago." Kelly said.

She took the statue from me and placed it back on the shelf where it belonged. I leaned in and continued looking, my hands behind my back.

"Zanks to dat cat, da little girl grew up to be quite a loved and respected woman," Kelly added.

"Cool. So are you Dutch or something? Is that how you know about that?"

"Yes." Doctor Kelly answered. "Or somezing."

"So is that your accent then?"

"Yes. Why? What did you zink it was?"

"I dunno, German or something."

Kelly laughed. "Well, it is a West Germanic language so I suppose I can see dat. Of course, English is, too. Do you know any odder languages, Travis?"

"Nope."

"Ahh, Americans and deir schools." She sighed. "In Holland we start speaking English at a very young age. Za Dutch speak many different languages. I've never understood why Americans are so satisfied wid just speaking one."

She watched intently as I continued to rummage through her things. Then in a low voice, more to herself than to me, she said, "I guess sometimes we all need a little help."

Doctor Kelly walked over to her desk and got a key out of the top drawer. "You know what? I have somezing you might like even better." She took the key over to a cabinet in the corner of the room.

I watched with curiosity as she unlocked the cabinet and pulled out a thin drawer lined with blue fabric.

"In fact, it might even help you." Doctor Kelly removed a black velvet pouch. "Dere's another legend," she said. "Dis one is even older."

"Is it Dutch, too?"

"It's kind of—everybody," she answered thoughtfully. Closing the cabinet, Kelly walked over to me and handed me the bag. "Dere is said to be a secret society," she explained, "called 'Da Lucid,' Who has found a way to escape all of da constraints of humanity. Dey are believed to have created deir own world—so whatever laws, uprisings, or challenges dey are ever faced with, dey can find solace."

"Where?" I asked. "Where is this world supposed to be?"

Doctor Kelly tapped the bag. "In zeir dreams."

I gave her a funny look and loosened the drawstrings. A dark green stone fell out into my hand. It had little red splotches on it and was hung with three small chains from a silver crescent that looked like the moon. The metal of the crescent looked very old, as if it had been pounded by hand.

"You made me zink of it when you mentioned your dreams earlier." Kelly said. "I zought you might appreciate it."

"What is it?"

"It's a talisman. According to legend, it was originally used by da Lucid as a gateway to da dream world."

"That's really cool," I said, "What's it got to do with me?"

"Talismans are very magical. Dey have da power to make extraordinary transformations. Why don't you keep it for a while? See how it works?"

"Oh, come on," I disagreed. "You don't really believe that, do you?"

Doctor Kelly smiled. "I believe very much in powerful transformations. Besides," she added with a wink, "bloodstones are supposed to be great healing stones—excellent for sleep problems." She took the talisman, dropped it in the bag, and handed it back to me.

It took a moment for me to realize what she was doing, but as it sunk in, I shook my head. "You're good." I said. "You're really good."

She laughed and patted my back. "So you'll try it?"

"Yeah, I'll try it."

The moment must have grounded me, which probably was all part of Doctor Kelly's plan. Because of this, I was actually able to sit back down and talk with her. We discussed the weather and my family—nothing big.

When I left, though, she asked me to be careful with the talisman.

I promised her I would, but really, I wanted to give it back. It seemed so old and so special, something that had great value to her. (It had its own locked space in her office, for Pete's sake!) I wondered if the talisman was worth a lot of money—a thought which instantly made me feel even worse.

You see, I didn't have a sleeping problem. I'd made the whole thing up. I just wanted something to talk about. That's the thing with therapists—they like to talk, and I had absolutely nothing going on in my life worth talking about. I chose a sleeping problem simply because it seemed like something that was hard to prove.

Little did I know that my lie and the doctor's talisman were about to make all of my dreams come true. And that as I began my walk home, I was about to run into the one person who (despite her own knowledge or wishes) was about to take that journey with me.

Chapter 3

She was the most beautiful girl I had ever seen. The most beautiful girl *the town of Everton* had ever seen. Her name was Corrine Johnson, but Corri is what her friends called her.

If only I could be named in that company.

Everton, Indiana, is small by big city standards, but not small enough where you absolutely know everyone in it. Although Corri and I are the same age, we go to different schools. With the myriad cliques and subcultures that come with adolescence, saying you go to different schools is pretty much the same thing as saying you live in different states. She probably recognized me with how often I visited her store. But we'd never had any kind of exchange long enough to be considered a real conversation.

And I was certain that Corrine Johnson didn't remember the first time we ever saw each other. Even though, for me, it was one of the defining moments of my life.

She had been thirteen and was walking with friends outside of the town library. The sun caught amber tones in her hair that day and the fiery tips made it look as though she were being illuminated from within, like the small white bags with candles that line our neighborhood streets at Christmas. She had this way of throwing her head back when she laughed that got her whole body involved. I'd never seen somebody laugh like that before.

As I walked past her on my way into the library, she smiled at me. I'm sure it was just a passing acknowledgment to her, but for me, the whole universe shifted. A charged light filled my entire being—for the first time, I felt completely alive.

I had witnessed perfection. And for a moment it had witnessed me—it had smiled upon me!

My heart began to pound as I neared the coffee house bookstore where she now worked. Every crack in the concrete was studied, counted, and memorized, so that without even lifting my head, I knew by the step how close I was to the entrance. A charming, familiar bell rang out as I pushed open the door.

That bell is as close to religion as I came.

"Hello!" Corri waved, then promptly turned her attention back to one of the coffeemakers behind the counter. She always had the same greeting and smile for everyone.

I said nothing in return, just quietly shuffled back to the metal book carousels on the other side of the store. Plucking a paperback from one of their shelves, I pretended to skim its pages. My breath quickened and went shallow at the realization that all that separated us were just a few cafe tables.

"Corri, can you make the regular first? I'm dyin' ova here!" Marissa came bounding out of the back kitchen speaking in a horrible, over the top, fake New York accent. She stopped and sighed when she saw me, as if someone let the air out of a balloon.

"Oh. Hey, Travis." After a beat and awkward stare she whipped back around to Corri, theatrics returning. "We had soooooo much fun last night. You really should have come out." Yanking the coffee pot out of Corri's hand, Marissa droned on about people I knew, doing things I never would. I let her voice fade into the background.

Unlike Corri, Marissa did go to my school. She was a year behind me, a self-proclaimed theatre nerd who was neither nice nor cruel to me. Everything about her was loud: her voice. Her makeup. Even her hair was loud—hard, black, sharp, and sprayed.

The two of them standing next to each other made for such a stark contrast. Taking advantage of their conversation, I summoned the courage to peer over the top of my book.

Corri was standing sideways, listening with a light smile on her lips. She never tried to look pretty; she just was. Her profile was perfect, with a delicate frame and flawless pale skin. Her shoulder length light brown hair had subtle waves in it, which you could still kind of see even though she usually tied it back at work. If she wore make-up, I couldn't tell. And almost every time I saw her, she wore blue jeans, a white t-shirt, and tennis shoes. I wondered what she looked like in a dress.

The bell above the door rang loudly and two forceful baritone voices ripped into my musings. "What's up, ladies?"

"Oh my God, John, I was just telling Corri how much fun we had last night!" Marissa leaned over the counter smacking her gum in what I could only assume was her attempt at being seductive.

His younger brother Terry stayed up front, but John bypassed Marissa immediately and walked a few steps down the counter so that he was opposite Corrine. I hated how tall he was. On a good day, I was 5'5". John must have had almost a whole foot on me.

Grinning, he used his strong forearms to prop himself up on the counter. "What's a guy gotta do to get you to go out with him, Corri?"

"I go out with you guys plenty," she answered, picking up a rag to wipe down the counters. "I'm not missing anything. We do the same old thing every time."

"I mean just you and me, Core. Whaddya say? When you gonna let me take you out?"

"Find someone your own age."

John snorted with laughter. "I've tried, but none of them's as pretty as you. Sides, I ain't that much older than you."

"I'm busy."

"I didn't say when."

"I'm not big into going out. I'd rather just stay in and read a book."

"A girl like you doesn't need to be stuck inside reading. You don't have any sense, girl!"

"I have enough sense not to get involved with the likes of you."

Without realizing it I let out a laugh from behind the book carousel. The room stopped.

Terry, who had been silent until now, asked, "Hey, who's back there?"

I sidestepped a bit, clutching my book to my chest.

"Who is that? I see you back there."

Terry was only a year younger than John and although they had similar features (perfect white smiles, blonde hair, and striking blue eyes), Terry was significantly smaller. But what he lacked in size, he more than made up for in bitterness.

"Thomas? That's your name right?"

I just held up my book as if that explained what I was laughing at, or what I was doing at the store in the first place. Looking down, I quickly walked over to the counter and put it down to pay.

Corri came over to the cash register, smiling politely and kindly.

Terry began to whistle some little nondescript tune as she did. The notes were all terribly off-key, but something told me that even if they weren't, I still wouldn't be able to make out the song.

"So you think Corri's funny, do ya Thomas?"

Terry stopped whistling and I could feel his eyes move over me as I pulled my wallet out of my back pocket.

"Leave him alone, Terry," she said. "It's nice to see you again. That'll be eighteen sixty-four." Corrine put her hand out for the money.

"What? I'm just askin'. You're funny. She's funny, right guys?"

Marissa and John chuckled.

Terry came closer to me. He leaned his back against the register crossing his arms and legs. He was so close I could feel his breath.

"She's real pretty, too, isn't she? You like looking at her?"

"Terry, knock it off."

My body, as I was so accustomed to, once again betrayed me. I willed it to stop, but the warmth had already moved up my spine and into my face as I handed Corri the twenty dollar bill.

"He's turning beet red! Oh my God look what you did, Corri! You didn't even have to touch him!" Terry roared. "You got this guy all hot and bothered. Just look at him!"

Everyone but Corrine erupted into laughter.

"Terry, I said knock it off!" She looked at me and smiled again. "Don't pay them any attention. They only just started walking upright." Corrine closed the register and handed me the change.

Calmly, she picked up the book. "I like Bill Bryson. This is one of my favorites." She leafed through a few pages of "A Walk in the Woods." "You know, he grew up in a small town like this? In Iowa."

All I could do was nod and look back down at the floor.

She smiled and handed it back to me.

Seeing her reaction, Terry now tried to put his arm around my shoulder. "Hey no hard feelings, kid. I was just kidding around. Just havin' some fun, OK?"

I wriggled out from under his arm and quickly hurried over to the door.

Corri must have given Terry a look because as the door closed behind me I heard him yell, "What? How was I supposed to know the guy was a mute?" Obviously he had forgotten my laugh was what had sparked the whole exchange.

None of that mattered, though. She had spoken to me. It was one of the most thrilling things that had ever happened. Not only had she spoken to me, but I was now holding something that was precious to her. "One of her favorites," she had said. I hadn't even looked at the title until she said that.

৪০৫৪

My strides were wide and fast, yet the concrete seemed to stretch and lengthen with every step.

I lived only a few short blocks down from the coffee shop, right above the laundromat my parents owned. Our building was three stories high. The bottom floor was completely devoted to the laundromat. The second floor was our living space, and until recently the top floor had been used only for storage.

My dad cleaned it out a few weeks ago. "Your first apartment" is what he called it. He was so excited when he first showed it to me. He and my mother presented it as an early graduation gift. They said it would give me more privacy—make me feel more independent.

I think they were disappointed by my reaction. It would have been any other seventeen-year-old's dream-come-true, but what did I need privacy for?

By the time I reached the building, I had broken into a full-fledged run. Bursting through the side entrance, I stumbled at the base of the stairs which led up to all three floors. I must have only touched down twice before reaching the top. In one swift movement, I made it through the door, across the room, and over to the modern gray fold-out couch I used as a bed.

I flopped down on my stomach, gasping for air. With the book in front of me, I used my feet to work off my shoes, and began reading. The book was about one man's quest to hike the entire length of the

Appalachian Trail. It was almost voyeuristic, imagining Corrine as she read, sharing in what must have been her reactions to the author's every triumph and defeat.

The idea of being somewhere she had been and feeling things she must have felt was so intoxicating that I couldn't let the story end. When I got to the last page, I refused to read it. Instead I went back a few chapters—just to make sure I hadn't missed anything. The next time I got to the last page, I flipped back to the beginning and started skimming through all of the chapters again—reliving passages at random.

This game went on for hours, during which my mother must have come up three or four times to ask me to come down for dinner. I told her I didn't feel well. She ended up leaving a half a sandwich and soup by the side of the bed.

Daylight retreated unnoticed and the food remained untouched.

When my eyes and body finally did succumb to the strain, I folded the second to last page and placed the book down next to me on the bed. I put my hand on its cover, as if swearing on a Bible, and vowed to save the end for a time when I really needed it.

Being in one position for so long had made my entire body stiff. I felt the soreness in every muscle as I carefully rolled onto my back and stared up at the ceiling. Every time I blinked, there was a bright flash of light and the ceiling appeared to get closer. Hoping to counteract the effect, I turned to the side.

That's when I felt the talisman. Its hard, round edges dug into my skin through the pocket of my jeans. I fished it out with my hand, and laid it out on the bed in front of me. The red flecks against the dark green of the stone looked like blood, but it was really quite beautiful. Flipping the talisman over, I discovered that there was a word carved into the back: dromencian.

I ran my finger over the deep groves of the letters, then groaned and fell back on the bed as a fresh new wave of guilt washed over me. If Doctor Kelly had really believed and cared enough to give me such a precious artifact, I least owed it to her to try one of her hippie therapies.

Placing the talisman on my forehead I closed my eyes. "Do your magic." I said sarcastically. Taking a deep breath, I laced my fingers together, and rested my hands on my stomach.

Over the next twenty minutes, I gradually felt my heart rate slow. As I concentrated on the rhythm of it, a warming sensation started at the crown of my head. It pulsed at the same speed as my heart and spread slowly, like honey, down the entire length of my body. Whatever tension there was in my muscles or care that existed in my mind completely melted away. It was extraordinary! An exquisite state of relaxation I never knew was possible.

Was I asleep? Was I awake?

Curious, I tried to open my eyes, but instead of seeing my room, my mind's eye was lit up with a few bursts of brilliantly colored light.

What was that?!

The flashes of light had startled me, but my body did not react. Willing myself to move, I was surprised to find that I no longer had control of my body. I was physically powerless, locked somewhere in this mysterious state between sleep and wakefulness.

This is certainly an odd situation to be in. I thought. Should I try to sleep or should I try to get up?

It didn't take more than a few seconds for me to come to the conclusion that being awake was nothing worth fighting for, so I let go. I surrendered myself fully and completely to whatever powerful grip this strange place of limbo had over me.

For a brief moment, I felt as if I was floating.

Then, just as my mind began to succumb to sleep, suddenly and without warning, the most unusual thing happened.

Chapter 4

I WATCHED HELPLESSLY AS AN OUTLINE STARTED TO APPEAR. THE SHAPE WAS foggy and grainy, but there was definitely something there; almost like a thin chalk outline had been etched on the inside of my eyelids.

Inside of an infinite darkness, I could only watch as the outline began to fill in far ahead of me in the distance. It was as if someone with a giant eraser was scrubbing away at the black background. There was no sound as a massive form took shape, and no frame of reference I could use to gauge time, which is why I don't know how long I stood there: seconds, maybe minutes? But it couldn't have taken very long before I realized what the outline was.

A mountain now stood against the inky blackness, towering far above my head. I had never seen anything like it, as it was a mountain made up entirely of massive stones. Snow dusted its jagged peaks, the same way it would if this were a real mountain.

I was completely transfixed by the magnitude of the image, but this odd experience wasn't over yet. A low rumbling began, like thunder far off in the distance. The noise became louder as it continued to roll and I started to feel a vibration in my feet. It moved up through my legs, to my stomach, and into my jaw, growing in intensity until I found I had to keep my mouth open to keep my teeth from clicking together. The sound of thunder became deafening. It was as though there were a thousand airplanes flying all around me in the dark—circling and diving all at once.

The area under my feet began to shake. Completely disoriented, I grasped blindly outward for something to hold onto. This is what an earthquake must feel like, I thought.

But instead of the ground falling away beneath me, it began to appear out of nowhere! First the grass, thick patches pushed under my feet. The life force of which knocked me to my knees.

Frightened, I reached out, grabbing huge fistfuls. I held on, frozen, as the grass spread out from under me in every direction at an unbelievable pace. Just before reaching the base of the mountain, the grass split apart and left a blank oval shape in its wake. There was a massive cracking sound overhead, followed by a blinding flash of light. Shielding my eyes, I crouched, defenseless, on the ground.

But what followed was even stranger yet: absolute silence. Everything stopped. The vibrations, the movement, the lights—everything.

Cautiously, finger by finger, I loosened my grip on the grass, and worked up enough courage to open my eyes. When I did, I found I had to squint as a yellow sun shone brilliantly above. It took a moment for my eyes to adjust, but as I lifted myself off the ground, everything came into focus.

My jaw dropped. I was somehow standing in the middle of an enormous field. Thousands of small purple and white flowers dotted the long blades of bright green grass. Up ahead, the field gave way to a small lake, a lake so still and so clear that it reflected a perfect mirror image of the mountains behind it. A breeze blew in, carrying with it the sounds of birds and insects chirping happily, and I felt the warmth of the sun on my face. White, wispy puffs of dandelion seeds floated through the air, which lent the landscape an ethereal quality.

As I took in the scene—its smells, sounds, and warmth—I knew something else had changed. After a moment, I figured it out–it was the colors here. They looked . . . different; more intense than usual. But somehow I knew it wasn't a difference in the actual colors– instead, it was a difference in me, in how I saw the colors. It was as if I had been blind my entire life and was truly seeing colors for the first time–pulsating, living, breathing colors.

I also became acutely aware of something else: I was dreaming.

I mean, I knew I was dreaming. Unlike normal dreams, I was entirely present. I knew all of the facts about my day. I even remembered reading just a short time ago. I stood there, in this dream, as myself, not as some drooling, subconscious amnesiac.

That made me realize what had just happened. As unbelievable as it was, I had just witnessed the formation of a dream. The formulation of my dream.

And it was beautiful. Completely untouched and unspoiled.

How had I come up with this particular landscape? My best guess was some vaguely-remembered scenes like this in a book I'd read, or maybe it was from a magazine advertisement.

I didn't travel, but this was definitely the kind of place I would go.

I took a few steps forward; as I did, tall grasses scratched lightly against my jeans. The sound startled me and I flapped my arms and legs about wildly. The comedy of the dance loosened me up a bit and taking in the perfect peaceful field around me, I had to laugh in spite of myself.

"As far as nightmares went, grass would have to rate pretty low on the terror scale," I thought, amused.

Feeling more confident, I took another step forward. "Hello?"

Nothing.

I took another step. This time I let out a yell. It was quiet, pitiful little sound, but there was something reassuring and powerful about hearing my own voice.

Next, I stretched my arms outward. Then I took in a deep breath, looked up to the heavens, and let out a resounding battle cry. The birds kicked up at the sound of my voice as it echoed across the great landscape.

This was unbelievable!

I laughed again and took another deep breath. This time I filled my lungs until they felt as though they would burst. But just as I opened my mouth to scream, a voice sounded from somewhere behind me.

"Hello?"

I jumped and turned around, choking on the air I had stored in my chest. Nothing could have prepared me for the shock of where that voice was coming from. Who that voice was coming from.

Standing there behind me, in a flowing white dress, was Corrine. "I didn't mean to scare you," she said.

Corri smiled, pursed her lips, and furrowed her brow. She had the oddest look on her face. It was a mixture of amusement and confusion.

I had never before seen an expression like that. I could do nothing but stare.

She looked at me for a response, then said, "I'm Corrine."

I was stunned. Struck absolutely deaf, dumb, and blind.

When I still didn't say anything, she grabbed my hand and shook it up and down in an overly dramatic pantomime. Mimicking the old Tarzan cartoons she said, "He-llo. Me Corr-ine. You?"

Jesus, I couldn't even remember my own name! I must have looked like such a moron.

She laughed. It was such a strange laugh, too. Not at all like what I had heard from her in the coffee shop. Then she looked past me at the water. "It's so beautiful." she gasped. "Is it real?"

I tried to look at the lake and the mountains, which had so fascinated me just moments before, but now found it nearly impossible to stare at anything but her.

"Can I help you?" she asked with a smile.

I shook my head with embarrassment and squeaked out, "Don't we know each other?"

Corrine turned to me and cocked her head to the side. "I don't think so. Should we?"

Her denial hurt. We didn't hang out, no, but we'd certainly seen enough of each other for her to at least recognize my face! Hadn't she herself said "it's good to see you again" when we talked at the coffee shop earlier in the day?

The coffee shop….

Corrine stood there awkwardly awaiting my response as my mind started to make the connection. Of course she didn't know me! The coffee shop was real–this was a dream. She was a figment of my imagination–granted a very detailed figment of my imagination, but she was part of the dream no less.

"It's a dream." I said out loud, both answering her original question and verbalizing my own thoughts.

She nodded, a kind of "thought so," and then looked back at the water. "It's incredible, isn't it?"

I followed her gaze and nodded in ironic dumbfounded agreement. She looked so real! Everything looked so real! I was going to have to work very hard to remind myself this was all a dream.

"You wanna go check it out?" she asked.

When I didn't say anything, Corrine gave my shoulder a quick slap. "Come on! Race ya!"

I reflexively grabbed my shoulder where she had hit me and watched as she lifted her dress off the ground. She wasn't wearing any shoes and I sucked in my breath at the sight of her bare feet and legs. Hiking her dress all the way up to her thighs and with the extra material gathered in both hands, Corri took off running full speed toward the water.

About halfway across the field, she stopped and looked back over her shoulder at me. I was frozen in place, still reeling from the unexpected glimpse of her perfectly shaped legs. "What are you waiting for?!" she called out. "Come on!" Her arm beckoned me to follow.

Without thinking, my body suddenly lurched forward. It moved completely on its own, an obedient dog jumping for its master.

When I reached her, she did the most amazing thing—she grabbed my hand. It was the first time a girl had ever touched me. The contact generated a cool kind of electric charge that surged throughout my whole body.

I wished she'd stop running so I could actually enjoy the moment. Instead, she dragged me all the way to the lake. When we got to the water, she still didn't stop—she ran right in without hesitation.

"Wait!" I cried.

Breathless from laughing and running, Corri grabbed my other hand so that she was now pulling me by both arms.

"I can't swim!"

"What?" Suddenly understanding, Corrine let me go.

Off balance, I rocked back, then toppled forward. The water splashed all around us as I first landed on her, then quickly rolled to the side. The shock of the cold water stunned us both. There we sat, our hands behind us, with sand-colored pebbles digging into our skin. We were side by side in six inches of water.

"It's freezing!" Corrine shouted.

My mouth fell wide open, but nothing would come out. The water felt like ice!

She took one look at my face and burst into hysterics.

I tried to jump up, to get out of it quickly, but the weight of the water in my clothes made me a clumsy, stumbling mess. I tripped more than a few times as I struggled to find the right footing, ending up with a comically-wide stance. But once I was truly confident I wasn't going to fall again, I reached out a hand to Corrine. It was one of the most chivalrous things I had ever done.

I felt a stir of childish superhero fantasy as my damsel in distress looked up and placed her hand in mine. She was still giggling as we climbed onto the bank and fell into a heap on the grass.

"Good thing the sun's warm, huh?"

I smiled back at her. The ice was broken, quite literally.

"You never told me your name." she said

"Travis. My name is Travis."

"Travis? That's a nice name. It's nice to meet you, Travis. I'm Corrine."

"I know."

"Oh, that's right, I told you that already, didn't I?"

I smiled back at her. She turned her head to the sky and I did the same, the grass folding like a gentle blanket under our backs. We lay silent like that for a long time, just watching the clouds float lazily overhead and enjoying the world around us.

After a while, Corrine looked down and pulled at her dress. "This thing's drying pretty fast."

"Um-hmm," I said noncommittally.

She plucked at the folds in the fabric. "What the heck am I wearing, anyway?"

"I always wanted to see you in a dress. I think that's why you're wearing it."

Corrine flipped onto her stomach and started pulling the petals off a flower in front of her. "You talk about me like you know me."

"Actually, we do know each other." I said.

"No, I'm pretty sure we don't. Believe me, I'd remember you." She stopped and her face flushed with embarrassment. "I didn't mean it like that."

"It's okay. I'm used to it."

Knowing it was all a dream, I felt oddly comfortable. I moved my hands behind my head and looked over at her. Corrine's hair was half up. A lock had fallen down and was softly brushing her cheek. "What are you like?" I asked

"What do you mean?"

"You're right," I said. "I don't know you."

With the flower between her fingers she made a graceful, sweeping circle with her wrist. "All of this around us and you want to know more about me?"

"Yes," I said. "I do."

"You're odd."

"We might not have much time."

"We may have forever." Corrine rolled on her side to face me and rested her head on her arm. "What do you want to know, Travis? Ask away."

"What do you like?" It's all I could think to ask.

"Oh, I don't know," she answered slowly. "The same things as everyone else, I guess. Simple things."

"Be more specific."

A sly, cocky smile crossed her lips. "If you wanted me to be more specific, you shouldn't have asked me such a general question."

"Okay, what do you want to be? What would you do, if you could do or be anything?"

She wasn't real, but it didn't matter. This was my chance to get all my burning questions answered, even if her answers were my own mind's interpretation of what she would actually say. I wanted to see straight into her heart—her hopes, her dreams, and her passions.

Corrine looked a bit hesitant. "I'd like to continue working where I work now," she said. "And I don't know, get married one day, ya know? Have kids and all of that."

I didn't say a word and waited for her to continue.

"What?" she asked.

"And?"

Corrine looked slightly annoyed, but also a bit embarrassed by my response. "And?"

"Oh, I'm sorry. I guess I thought there was more. Were you done?"

"I mean, I'd like to maybe take some art classes or take some cool vacations one day…." She paused, obviously irritated at having to defend her life's ambitions. "Why? What about you? What are *your* grand plans?"

"For me, it doesn't matter," I said. "I never give it any thought." It was my turn to be cocky now.

"Oh, yeah? Well, sure, yeah, I guess that whole dream person, not existing thing, would kind of get in your way, huh?"

She thought *I* wasn't real? Part of *her* dream? That was rich! I thought about Doctor Kelly and how she'd have a field day with what this probably had to say about my subconscious.

I turned on my side to face her, our bodies perfectly mirroring each other now. "All I'm saying is—you have this great sense of humor. You're smart. You're beautiful. You could do or be anything you want."

"Well, thank you for saying that, but what if a happy family life *is* what I want? Why does everyone feel this need to prove themselves, anyway? What's so threatening with just being happy with who you are?"

"Doesn't doing great things make people happy?"

"Great things? Who are they great for? They're great for impressing *other* people, that's who."

"I don't know about that."

"Do you want me to be a doctor? I can be a doctor. It's just school," she said. "Or would being a workaholic lawyer make my quality of life any better?"

I thought about this; it made sense.

Corrine finished with, "A job title alone shouldn't determine my worth."

"No," I agreed, hoping I hadn't offended her too greatly. "But I suppose it does help someone to get to know you better. To know what you like. Know what your interests are. That's all I'm saying."

She stopped and stared at me a moment. "I'm sorry." She took a deep breath and I could see her shoulders relax. "I guess I'm a bit defensive when it comes to that kind of stuff."

"Why?"

"I don't know. I just feel like everyone's always judging everyone else," she said. "And, well, I guess I'm just sick of people always talking down to me."

Corrine averted her gaze and cleared her throat while she brushed at non-existent grains of sand on her arm. "I mean, I work at a coffee shop, yeah. But you know what? I like it. I like books. I like the smell of them. I like the quiet too. People treat me like they have me all figured out. Like I'm some sort of stupid small town bimbo just because I don't want to go to college."

"Wow," I said, taking it all in. "That's weird."

"What's weird?"

"I always imagined people would have nothing but nice things to say to you."

Corrine shot up, crossed her legs, and leaned forward. "There you go acting like you know me again! Geez, Travis, I'm starting to think you're just as bad." She laughed as she said this so that I knew she was teasing me. "Sometimes I think I should just go ahead and climb Mount Everest."

I followed her lead and sat up. Stretching my legs out in front of me, I leaned back on my arms. "So, is that something you want to do then?"

"No. It's just that way, when people ask what I do, I can say yeah, I work at a coffee shop, but I did climb Mount Everest once."

"With your bare hands," I added.

"Blindfolded!" she giggled.

"Yeah, that'll show em." Corri's laughter trailed off. "Wow, this conversation got really serious really fast, didn't it? Do you do this with all the girls you meet?"

"You're actually the first girl I've ever talked to."

Corrine swatted my leg. "You're so odd," she said again, laughing. "Nah, it's cool. I'm having a good time. Thanks."

I felt myself blush and looked down at the grass.

Corrine started to say something else but abruptly stopped. "Travis?"

"What?"

"Travis, what's happening?"

"What do you mean?"

She was staring at my shoulder and when I followed her gaze I noticed that my arm had become somewhat translucent. I tried to move it, but found I had no control.

"I can't move my arm," I said, bewildered.

Corri looked at me first for approval, then tentatively extended her hand into the empty space where my shoulder had been. A look of amazement washed over her. "I can't feel anything either!" she gasped. "What does it feel like? Does it hurt?"

"No. It doesn't feel like anything."

We watched curiously as my arm completely disappeared in front of us.

"Look!" Corrine pointed to my leg. The phenomenon had moved to my foot. My toes and my ankle on my right side were dissolving just as my arm had; the grass and the flowers popping back up where the weight of my body had once kept them down.

When all but the top of my leg had vanished I realized what was happening.

It was ending.

My mind raced; there was so much more I wanted to say to her, but I could actually physically start to feel myself being pulled away from this fantastic, unconscious world.

"Corrine. Before this is over, I have to tell you something."

She leaned in as if I were about to share some profound truth with her.

Her eyes were wide, which allowed me to notice for the first time just how strangely beautiful they were. They weren't brown as I had thought. They were filled with hundreds of gold and red flecks, and looked like fire. Her eyelashes were huge, wide fans. As she blinked, I watched each individual lash fall in slow motion. It made me think of a beautiful silk curtain falling on a wooden stage.

"This was the best day of my entire life," I whispered.

She leaned her head to the side and smiled the sweetest smile I had ever seen. A shadow crossed her face and Corrine scooted toward me on the ground until we were just inches apart.

I opened my mouth to say more, but nothing would come out. She touched a finger to my lips as if to quiet me. And although I could see her mouth moving, I was no longer able to hear her.

Corrine brought her face close to mine and scanned my eyes as if deciding what to do next.

She leaned in...

That's where it stopped. Everything went black.

I never felt her.

Chapter 5

When my eyes opened, I was on my back with my arms by my sides. I stayed in that position, blinking and expressionless. A stunned fish ripped from its sea, its gills moving only out of habit.

I had left the blinds open. Bright light poured in through the window; it lit dust particles in the air. I watched as my breathing made them swirl and change direction over my head. My shoes were on the floor where I had kicked them off and I was still in yesterday's clothes.

As the room slowly registered, I stretched out my hand and made a fist. I did this a few times. When it was absolutely clear I had control over my body again, I reached for a pillow at the top of the bed, pulled it to my face, and screamed.

The strong scent of fabric softener immediately invaded my mouth and nose. I pulled the pillow away from me, choking. Corrine's face burned in my mind.

That's when it hit me. "The talisman!"

I sat up like a shot. Tearing through the sheets, I found the talisman buried beneath the comforter at the base of the bed.

My eyes were as wide as saucers as I held it up in front of my face. It didn't look any different.

It couldn't be, I thought. Did the talisman work? Had I just entered some kind of secret dream world?

I flipped it over a few times and stared at it as if waiting for something "magical" to happen. When it didn't, I laughed quietly to myself.

"Nah. No way," I muttered. It was all too fantastical.

Chuckling at myself, I leaned over and shut the talisman away into the nightstand beside my bed. As I closed the drawer, I noticed the time on my alarm clock.

9:15 a.m. The neon red numbers brought reality crashing back. "Shoot! I'm late!" I yelled.

I leaped from the bed and ran to a small, makeshift eating area in the corner of the room. It consisted of two oak chairs and a matching dinette table, on top of which sat a stainless steel coffee maker and (courtesy of my mom) a big light blue vase filled with faded fake sunflowers. There was still some coffee in the pot from yesterday. I poured it into my favorite mug and grabbed a toaster pastry out of a nearby box.

My dad had put in a bathroom for me in what had been the old storage closet across the hall. I ran over and quickly checked myself out in the full length mirror that hung behind the door. "Not too bad." I used my hands to flatten out my shirt and hastily ran my fingers through my wild black hair. As I did, I noticed a big fresh zit on my forehead and tried valiantly to cover it back up again. "Guess that'll have to do."

Hurrying back into my bedroom in a dramatic fashion, I flung myself into the chair of my small computer desk. "Good thing I'm close to work."

Chuckling at my own joke, I held my mug up in a mock toast. I bit into the toaster pastry and took a sip of cold coffee.

I had found myself an online job for the summer. I was doing data entry for a large health care company. It wasn't much, but it was the source of some pride. I felt purposeful.

Since I worked from home, I didn't have a true schedule. I mean, I didn't have to clock in anywhere, but it was routine and I liked routine. You could rely on routines. Customs and rituals were the closest things to friends I had.

But on this day, my friends did not seem too fond of my company. The clock became more like my enemy as I mindlessly pecked away at the keyboard. I couldn't stop thinking about Corrine—about what she might be doing. I pictured her in the white dress, her hair in her face, plucking at the petals on the flower.

It was as if there were two of her now. The one I had gotten to know in my dream, and the mysterious one that worked at the coffee shop.

My typing gradually slowed, then stopped. At one point I caught myself staring at the blinking cursor on the screen for what must have been at least ten minutes. This was ridiculous, I thought. How was I ever going to get anything done like this?

Her face consumed my every thought. Just to know she was going about her day would somehow make me be able to go about mine, I resolved.

Turning off the computer, I leaned over and grabbed my shoes. I picked up the book I had bought the day before, to use as a talking point in case I needed one, and headed out.

There was an unseasonable chill in the air as I stepped onto the street. Above, the Washington Hawthorns were in full bloom; from my door to the coffee house and beyond, their delicate white blossoms lined the entire length of Main Street.

Unlike most cities its size, Everton's downtown is truly functional. Main Street is its heart. Clothing stores, sandwich shops, and hip pubs featuring weekly Karaoke breathe life into its 1950's charm. There are apartments, single family homes, and offices off of it, but the "downtown," also known as Main Street, is really only a couple of blocks long.

It's one of the last great towns where everyone is equal. All of the neighborhoods are middle class, their modest homes well-kept with fresh paint and manicured lawns. Old trees line just about every street, making it feel lived-in and safe. Like life always had been, and always would be, this simple.

There are many schools, but they are all housed in buildings that don't look like schools. My high school, for example, looks like an old stone church, the front of which showcases a large copper spire with a magnificent working clock inside.

Although Everton is an ideal place to raise children, it doesn't offer much in the way of keeping them around. There are no colleges to speak of, and after high school, most kids leave town to follow their dreams.

As I approached the coffee house, I went to zip up my grey hoodie, but stopped as I realized with embarrassment that I was still wearing the same clothes as the day before. I couldn't let her see me in the same clothes. It was an awkward kind of dance as I tried to decide whether or not to go inside.

Then, through the window, she appeared. Corrine was carrying an armful of books to the front of the store. She had a huge smile on her face. Although I couldn't hear through the glass, it looked as though she was singing. She was so caught up in whatever she was listening to, or whatever it was that she was thinking about, that she didn't once seem to notice me standing in front of the window. For a moment, I let myself believe I was the reason for her distraction.

I watched with amusement as she carefully and methodically set out new hardbacks on the wooden display shelf. You could tell just by the way she handled them how much she cared about the stories inside. As the normalcy of the task sank in, so did the absolute absurdity of me being there. Corrine was going on about her life and I was watching life from the outside. She was like a beautiful butterfly inside of a glass case, and I was the grubby kid who leaves nothing but fingerprints behind, imagining what it's like to actually touch something so perfect.

Nothing had changed

Satisfied with my mission and the acceptance of our respective roles, I took one more appreciative look and turned to go. But as I did, I realized that someone had been watching me while I had been watching her. Leaning against the street corner was Terry. He was smoking a cigarette.

He and John worked at a bar just a few doors down that their uncle, Art, owned. They were there all the time, so I shouldn't have been surprised to see him. Terry and John might not have gone on to do anything worthwhile after high school, but working at one of the only bars in a small town ensured they'd never lose their "life of the party" status.

Terry raised a hand and wiggled his fingers slowly. It would have been a harmless gesture had it given by anyone else, but something about the way he did it felt threatening.

With one hand still holding the book I'd brought with me, I dug my free hand deep into my pocket and picked up my pace.

He said nothing as I passed him. He just smiled like a wolf, his head moving with me. As I crossed the street, I could hear him start to whistle another one of his creepy little tunes.

What was it about him and whistling?! The sound was so unnerving! It made every hair on my body stand on end. I kept my eyes glued to the ground the whole rest of the way home. When I got to my room, I moved around in an endless methodical circle—from the computer, to the table, to the bed where I'd watch TV, then back to the computer.

It wasn't until around six-o-clock that night that I finally made my way downstairs for dinner, where I dutifully pushed peas around my plate as my parents droned on about business. "May I be excused?"

"What? You're still not feeling well?" my mom asked.

I shrugged. "I just want to take a shower and lie down."

My mom reached across the table and put a hand on my forehead. "You feel all right," she said. "Do you want me to call the doctor?"

I pushed her hand off me and scooted back from the table. "I'm fine, Mom. Geez, I just want to lie down. Why is that such a big deal?"

"I was just asking."

"Teenagers," my Dad grunted.

"Parents," I huffed back.

Leaving my food on the table, I stormed off down the hall to the bathroom. There was a radio on the back of the toilet. I cranked up the volume and locked the door behind me.

It felt good to be alone.

Discarding my clothes on the floor, I opened the shower, pushed the handle to its coldest setting, and stepped in. I clasped my hands in front of my face and let the cold water rush over my body. Shivering, I leaned against the cracked tiles, trying desperately to bring back the image of Corrine laughing in the icy lake.

Sleep did not come easily that night. Ironically, I experienced my first real bout of insomnia. "Karma," my Mom would have said had she'd known the trick I pulled on poor Doctor Kelly.

I leaned over and reached into the drawer on my night stand. Pulling the talisman from its bag, I hesitated for a moment, before placing it under my pillow.

It felt a bit silly, but . . . it couldn't hurt, I'd thought.

I couldn't have been more wrong.

It was black and the rumbling was there again. This time though, it passed quickly. My hair and clothes moved about me in the dark and little grains of sand swept across my face, finding their way into my mouth and crunching between my teeth. I had the strangest sensation of moving through a tunnel. Unlike the last time, I could already feel the world around me in the dark. The air was cool and moist and something that felt like gravel moved beneath my feet.

Spreading out from where I stood a light began to illuminate the landscape. Shadows retreated at a smooth even pace and were replaced by the rosy glow of sunrise.

With my surroundings lit, I could now see where I was. I was standing on a dirt road, deep in the woods. It was a wide path, the color of wet sand. White and grey rocks of various sizes were scattered about. Dense forest framed both sides. The tops of the tall trees bowed inward so their branches formed a sort of canopy over where I stood. Mossy grass and dark green ferns spilled out from the forest floor and crept along both sides of the road.

The dirt path split in two about thirty feet in front of me. A giant, gnarled tree marked the divide. The trunk was as wide as I was tall, and its branches were twisted into shapes that told of centuries of abuse from some of history's worst storms. In front of the tree, right where the road forked, someone was sitting cross legged on the ground. It appeared to be a young woman, but her back was to me so I couldn't tell who she was.

I took a step forward. A few stones moved under my feet, making a noise that drew the woman's attention. When she turned around, my heart skipped. It was Corrine.

She looked over her shoulder at me and beamed, but did not get up. Instead, she shot her hand into the air and waved me toward her. In front of her, in her lap, she was holding something that seemed to be of great excitement.

I skipped a step and hurried over to her in a light jog. "Hi!"

She said nothing immediately, but yanked my arm so that I fell on my knees next to her.

"Look!" she exclaimed. In her hand was a tiny, bright yellow bird. Its feathers appeared to be made out of a million little scales that sparkled and reflected the light like sequins. The bird just sat there calmly looking straight ahead.

"Wow, I've never seen anything like it," I said. "Can I touch it?"

"Sure, go ahead."

Corrine opened her hand wide and I touched my index finger to the back of the bird. The scales were very hard but smooth to the touch. It was the coolest thing!

But as its eyes turned up to me, I felt my stomach drop. The bird's eyes were made of stone! They were dark green with blood red spots—exactly the same as the talisman.

"Isn't it amazing?!" she exclaimed. "I made it!" Corrine swelled with pride at the proclamation.

"You made what?" I stammered, trying to collect myself.

"Here, I'll show you how it works." With the bird cupped in one palm, she took one of my hands with her own and placed it over the bird. "Think of something," she whispered.

"What?"

"Close your eyes, and concentrate really hard on something. Think of anything you can hold in your hand."

I gave her a sideways stare and reluctantly closed my eyes.

"Are you thinking of something?" she asked.

"Give me a second," I said. It was hard to think about anything except her hand on top on my own. It was intoxicating-the warm sensation of where our skin made contact, the spaces between her fingers. I could hear her inhale and exhale, and I knew without even looking at her that her eyes were closed as well.

I had visited a place like this once as a child. My parents had rented a cabin way up north, deep in the woods. All I could remember about that trip was fishing in a canoe and catching tree toads that hopped in and out of the clover in front of our cabin door.

"Are you ready?" she asked.

I opened my eyes and shrugged. "I guess."

She lifted my hand with her own.

My mouth fell open. Because the bird was gone! And in its place, sitting squat in the palm of her hand was now a tiny tree toad. "How did you do that?!"

"I didn't," she said. "You did." Corrine opened her fingers and delicately released the toad onto the path. It hopped a few times, hesitated a moment, then changed direction so that it had a more direct path into the woods. It was as if it had always been there.

"Come on!" she said as she popped up, pulling me with her. "Let's do more!"

We ran around the forest touching leaves—changing their colors from green, to orange, to brilliant blues that would never occur in nature. It was spectacular. We were the mystical rulers of an enchanted forest.

At one point, as I was willing a lizard on a tree to have spots, I called over to her. "So how did you figure this out, anyway?"

Corrine was standing over a sapling watching it grow up and out of the earth toward her. "All of this," she said, waving her hand to suggest the entirety of the scene around us, "is an illustration of The Road Not Taken. Robert Frost? The poem, you know? This is the screen-saver on my computer."

I moved toward her. "I'm not sure I'm following."

"Well, I just figured if my mind made this picture, why couldn't it change it, too?" She twirled around and did a curtsey. A big pink butterfly was on her shoulder. She brought her chin down toward it and smiled.

I laughed. I couldn't help myself. "You are completely adorable."

My own admission caught me off guard. I rubbed the back of my neck and laughed nervously.

She laughed too, but our laughter soon gave way to an awkward silence.

Maybe a bit too enthusiastically I asked, "So, where do these paths go, anyway?"

Corrine seemed to shake off a chill. Oddly enough, I couldn't tell if she was thankful for the diversion, or not.

"In the poem, I think they both led to the same place," she said.

"Which one are you supposed to take?"

"That's the thing. Robert Frost wrote that he was a better man for taking the path less traveled. So I guess—that one."

She pointed to the path on the right. It had a dark, foreboding look about it. The one on the left, as far as I could see, seemed bright and well-worn.

I stood next to Corrine and we looked down the darker path together. "Where do you think it goes?" I asked.

"There's only one way to find out."

Chapter 6

The woods appeared to get thicker with every passing minute as we walked purposefully along the path less traveled. The dense brush blocked out the sun, creating the illusion of night. The creatures of the forest called out to each other in the dark and tiny orbs of white light floated in and out of the trees.

"It's kind of spooky, isn't it?" Corrine said, stepping closer to me.

I looked around and frowned, not agreeing or disagreeing.

She looked at me, and continued to stare, as we walked silently side by side. I would occasionally glance over at her but for the most part pretended not to notice.

"You know, you're not like other guys," she finally said.

With all the distractions and excitement of the dream, I had completely forgotten who I was in the real world. It seemed now even my own subconscious felt the need to remind me that there was nothing normal about me sharing my company with a woman like Corrine.

"Yeah, well we all have faults," I said.

Leaves and larger sticks were beginning to litter our path and the underbrush was spilling out onto the road. I pointed to a large branch she was about to walk into. "Watch out!"

"Thanks," Corrine said as she stepped over it. "Why do you act like I'm saying that in a bad way?"

"Well, aren't you?"

I never considered she could be paying me a compliment.

"No, I just mean you don't act like most of the guys I know. But that's a good thing," she added. "I like it."

"How's that?" There was no hiding the shock in my voice.

Corrine moved in front of me and pulled a tree limb that was at face level out of my way.

"Thanks."

"Hey, one good turn deserves another, right?" She walked backwards a few steps, then spun back around on her heels.

I tried to follow her as best I could, but the narrow path we were walking on was becoming increasingly harder to navigate.

"Like right now," Corri continued. "You're letting me lead the way. Other guys would try to be all macho and treat me like I didn't know what I was doing."

"Why?"

"Exactly. I don't know either."

We turned a slight corner and came upon a huge tree that had fallen across the entire width of what was left of the trail. Corrine didn't hesitate and climbed right up. She paused at the top, waiting for me, straddling the log.

"I don't know why anyone would give you a hard time," I squeaked as I struggled to meet her. "You're perfectly capable."

"Thanks, Trav." She patted the log under us and effortlessly slid down the other side.

My dismount was not as graceful. I fell like a sack of rocks, arms and legs flailing. I acted surprised about the faulty landing but was actually kind of amazed I had gotten up there at all.

She laughed as she helped me to my feet. "I like you, Travis, and that's saying a lot. I really can't stand a lot of people."

"You can't stand people?"

"Hate 'em." She looked over her shoulder at me, wrinkled her nose, and smiled.

"Well, I hate 'em too, then." I liked the feeling of agreeing with her.

"Oh, yeah? Tell me why you hate people, Trav." Her back was to me, but her voice got louder with the challenge and I could hear her smile.

I thought about it a second. After the tree, the path had become all but lost, and it was getting much harder to make our way through. "I dunno. I guess because of the power they have," I said, leaning down to grab a stick off the ground.

"You're gonna have to explain that one!" she called back.

"It's like they can say whatever they want, whenever they feel like it, ya know?" I used my stick to hit some branches out of the way as I went on. "They don't care. And it doesn't matter how you react. It doesn't matter if you ignore them. Whatever you do, you can't stop people from affecting you–from changing you in some way."

Corrine stopped and whipped around to face me. Her smile was completely gone. She opened her mouth to speak, but I interrupted before she could. "Oh, my God! Look! We made it!"

Corrine looked around, confused.

I pointed over her shoulder. "We made it!" I yelled again. "Look!" I moved past her to the clearing.

Just about twenty feet in front of us, light was hitting a patch of clear ground just outside of the woods. The vegetation of the forest acted as a kind of curtain; the clearing was only visible from where it stopped, maybe a foot off of the ground. We were going to have to duck under all of those tangled branches to get to it.

"Come on!" I took the lead, and hurried over to the edge of the forest. Thorny vines weaved in and out of tree limbs and I got a nasty scratch on my hand as I lifted them up. "Be careful."

Corrine nodded, and crouched down to crawl through the opening I had created. I ducked and scooted my way out behind her.

As she stood up, Corrine was the first to see where we were. "Whoa!"

I stepped around her to see what she was looking at, and the view nearly knocked the wind out of me. We were standing on a cliff hundreds of feet up in the air. It jutted out over a vast, wooded terrain. Lush green mountains stretched out in every direction below us. The cliff itself was bald and the smoothness of the ground was a welcome relief.

I took a step forward, finding it hard to keep my footing. The height was dizzying.

"So which one of us do you think made this?" Corrine asked. Her voice was filled with awe.

I turned my back on the view to face her. "Wait a second," I said. "Something isn't adding up."

"What do you mean?"

"You said the woods were the screen-saver on your computer, right?"

"Yeah."

"But that doesn't make any sense...." I kicked at the reddish dirt with my feet and began to pace. "If this is my dream—how can you be the one controlling it?"

She mirrored my movement so that we circled each other, like two boxers in a ring. "Who said this was your dream, Travis?"

"Well, it has to be somebody's, doesn't it?"

Corrine stopped and slowly nodded, indicating that she understood. "So the question you're asking is—which one of us is the real one? Right?"

"Riigght." I agreed slowly, letting it sink in. I honestly hadn't realized that was what I was asking her until she said it back to me.

Corrine threw her hands up in the air. "Well that's easy. It's me. After all, I did make the woods and I was the one who figured out how to change things, too."

I shook my head. "No. That can't be right."

"Did you make this?" Corrine asked, sweeping her hand to signal the cliff and mountains.

"No."

"Well then, there's your answer. It must be me." She seemed quite confident with her conclusion.

"This isn't your dream, Corrine."

"Oh, really?" She crossed her arms in front of her body defensively. "Please, go ahead. Since you seem to be the expert, why don't you enlighten me, Travis? Why don't you tell me why this isn't my dream?"

"I know this isn't your dream," I said, stepping in her direction. "because if you were real, then you'd know who I am."

Corrine gave me a perplexed look. "What does that mean?"

"It means I know who you are. I know where you work. I live in your town. I see you all the time and I know this is my dream, because if I ever had the ability to control any kind of dream—YOU are what it would be about!" The words spilled from my lips like water. I clasped my hand to my mouth, instantly wishing I could shove everything back in.

The confession obviously caught her off guard. Corrine swallowed hard, taking a moment to collect her thoughts.

I could feel my body start to tremble. My cheeks burned like fire. "I'm sorry," I said, taking my hand off my mouth. "I didn't mean—"

She moved toward me.

I reflexively tried to take a step back, but she kept coming.

Corrine grabbed my shirt by the chest and pulled me to her. Her arms shot up and locked around my neck. Then she did the most extraordinary thing: she kissed me.

She kissed *me*.

Her body was warm and soft against mine, and the sweet, sticky taste on my lips was like nothing I had ever experienced.

I had no idea what to do. At first, I just stood there like a statue. Then, I don't know if natural instincts kicked in or what, but my hands moved around her waist and I pulled her closer.

Adrenaline coursed through my body. My arms felt strong. I was kissing her back. It was confusing, exhilarating, scary, and wonderful all at the same time.

Corrine's breathing quickened and she pushed against my chest to break the hold.

Not wanting to let go, I grabbed at her waist again, but she stopped me.

"What did you do that for?" I asked, my voice low and raspy. Even I couldn't tell if I was asking why she kissed me or why she had stopped.

Corrine stepped back even further and looked down at her legs.

That's when I saw it. The shin of her left leg was starting to fade.

"Travis, I don't know you," she said softly. "If this is real, though? If it's really real, like you say it is? I want to meet you. Do you understand me? I want you to come and find me as soon as you wake up."

The light around us changed. It was sunset. Amazing reds, golds, and purples, streaked across the sky.

I started to try and ask her where we should meet and when, but she didn't want to hear it.

"Don't," she said, turning her head to the sunset. "I don't want to talk anymore. Just stand here with me until I wake up. I want to enjoy this."

I understood exactly what she meant. Nodding, I silently took my place beside her. We looked out over the cliff, the wind blowing about our hair and clothes. I grabbed her hand and she squeezed mine back.

I wanted to stare at her. I wanted to discover all of the new and unexplored details of her face that I had never dared to try to find before. But I couldn't bear the thought of watching her fade away, so I kept my face to the sky. Only once the warmth of her hand had disappeared from my own, and I was absolutely sure that she was gone, did I walk to the edge of the cliff.

I screamed as loud as I could, "I love you!"

And I could have sworn, somewhere above me in the sky, or around me, or in my head, I heard her whisper it back.

Chapter 7

The phone was ringing as I opened my eyes to the real world. I didn't have a cell phone. I barely had a landline. I didn't know what it would even feel like to actually need call waiting, caller ID, or any of the other basic functions that most people take for granted.

I picked up the receiver on the floor next to my bed, knowing it could only be one of two people. "Hello."

"Hey, honey. I'm so sorry—did I wake you up?" My mom's voice was sweet and sing-songy. She had always been a morning person. For her the world was a place worth waking up to; every day full of promise and new adventures.

"Yeah, but it's okay, Mom." I got out of the bed and made my way over to the closet, the cordless cradled between my shoulder and my ear. The phone had been a present from my mom—my own phone with my own line, to go with my very own "apartment."

"Well, I wanted to catch you before you started working," she said. "Your father and I were thinking about going out for breakfast. We thought you might like to come down and join us."

"I can't, Mom." I raked through the few shirts I had hanging in the closet.

"Well, it's Friday and I just thought it would be a nice way to end the week."

"Uh huh." I moved to the shelves and pulled out some shirts, laying them on the bed. I hoped that I had at least imagined a better wardrobe for myself in the dreams.

"Travis? You sound distracted, honey. Is everything okay?"

"Mom, I have to go. I have stuff to do."

"Well, we're not going to go for long if that's what you're thinking."

"Hey, bud. So we're doing breakfast today, are we?" My dad's voice now joined my mom's on the phone. This is how they liked to talk to me when they called. They each have their own cordless in their apartment, too.

Isn't that cute? We're just one big cordless family.

"No, Dad. I was just telling Mom I'm busy today. I have to go meet someone."

"Oh, really? Who is that?"

"No one. Just this girl." I regretted the words the moment they left my mouth.

There was silence on the other line for a moment.

"A girl? What girl?" My mother did a decent job of trying to contain the excitement that I knew was oozing out of her every pore.

"Nobody. It's nothing. It's just a school thing."

"School thing? What school thing? School's out, isn't it?" my dad asked.

"Oh, Travis." my mother sighed. "You don't have to make up something from the year, do you?"

"Make up something? What does that mean?" my dad asked.

Before I could even answer my mom said, "It was math, wasn't it? I just knew we should have gotten you a tutor. I knew it."

"Math? You failed a math class, Trav?" My dad's questions now started to overlap my mom's.

It's amazing how parents can take one line and completely invent an entire back story that doesn't exist. "Mom, dad, stop. My grades are fine. I'm just going to meet this girl to help her with something from *her* school. That's it."

"Well, that doesn't make sense, Travis. What's this girl have to do with your math class?" my dad asked.

"There's nothing wrong with my math class! I got a B+, Dad! Look, I'm just busy. Go eat breakfast. Have fun. I'll be down when I'm done working. I have to go, okay?"

They started to say more but I quickly said, "I love you, goodbye," and hung up the phone.

"Huh." I put my thumb under my chin and examined the clothes laid out before me. A bright orange tee-shirt with a dragon on its right side caught my eye. I had never worn it. I didn't know much about fashion, but my aunt, who sent it to me a couple of years ago, lived in a big city so I figured she knew more about style than I did. I set it aside along with my favorite pair of old jeans.

I spent more time getting ready than I had in my entire life. While brushing my teeth, I practiced things to say to her and got toothpaste all over the mirror. I washed myself two or three times over in the shower and combed my hair until it was almost completely dry, which set each strand into a perfect molded shape. Thank goodness I had no hair on my face to shave, or maybe I never would have left the house at all. I put on the dragon shirt and jeans and rummaged through old Christmas boxes in the closet until I found the finishing touch I was looking for—a bottle of cologne. I'd never used cologne before, and choked on the mist as I sprayed myself.

I looked at myself one more time in the mirror and grabbed the book I had bought two days before. This was it.

I took a deep breath, nodded, and walked out.

It was as if I had carried the confidence out of the dream with me. With my head up, I walked straight to the coffee house, unwavering and unafraid. When I got to the door, I could see Terry and John talking to Marissa and Corri through the window. The idea of them being there didn't shake me at all. She was waiting for me.

I threw open the door, held my chest high, smiled, and looked right at Corrine. I planted my feet, taking a stance that said, "I have arrived."

The conversation halted and they all looked at me with startled expressions. "Umm, can I help you?" Corri asked.

My heart fell into my stomach and my confidence shattered around me like glass as she greeted me with the same expression and smile she always did.

What an idiot! How could I have thought it was real? My legs began to wobble and I felt the heat in my face.

Marissa, John, and Terry snickered.

"Well, what is it? What do ya want?" Marissa asked.

"I, uh—" I stammered. I wanted to be anywhere but here. "I, um—just came to look for another book by this guy." I shook the book in my hand.

Corrine stood up. "Oh, yeah. You bought that Bill Bryson book the other day, right? Sure, I remember. There's one called A Short

History of Nearly Everything. It should be on that back shelf there." She got up on her tiptoes and stretched her arm high in the air, pointing to the very back corner of the store.

Her voice made a lump rise in my throat.

"Back there," she reiterated when I failed to move.

I swallowed hard, hoping to hold back the sobs, which threatened to break at any moment.

Corri quieted down everyone's laughter.

I moved to the back of the store and just looked at the shelf.

How could I have been so foolish?

"Nice shirt," Terry said it loud enough so I could hear. Marissa and John laughed in unison.

What was I doing? How did I get myself into this mess? There was only so much humiliation even I could take.

I had to get out of there. Not wanting to walk directly past them, I scurried along the side of the wall like a mouse.

Terry called out to me just as I reached the door. "Hey! Thomas! Too bad you're going. You're gonna miss Corri's new mystery boyfriend. She says he's stopping by today."

I felt a shiver go all the way from my toes up to the top of my head.

Terry walked over to me and put a hand on my shoulder in a fake show of support.

"Yeah, she thinks she's in love. She says they went hiking in the woods somewhere or something. Sorry, man. Looks like you missed out on your chance with—"

I knocked his hand off me and whipped around to look at Corrine. "It's me!" I cried out. "Travis! The lake? The woods? It's me!"

Her eyes widened. What I saw in them made me want to drop to my knees. She knew who I was! I could see it. She recognized me! It was real.

"The bird! You made the bird!" I bellowed. "It was yellow and its eyes were made of stone!"

Corrine shook her head back and forth in disbelief. As I staggered toward her, she tripped backwards and fell into the line of coffee pots behind her.

"What the? Grab him!" I heard John yell.

In all the excitement I had forgotten there were other people in the room.

"The guy's gone nuts!" Terry screamed.

I felt their arms grab me from behind.

Marissa, who had been watching the scene unfold in stunned silence, now ran to Corri to help her to her feet. "Get him outta here!" she yelled.

John and Terry started to pull me back by the shoulders. I swung around and hit Terry square in the face. The smacking sound that my hand made against Terry's cheek shocked them enough to let me go for a second.

The enormity of what I had just done didn't register at all.

I rushed forward, completely out of control. But as I got closer to Corri, her image started moving away from me. Terry and John had lifted me clear off the ground. They were carrying me by my arms, backwards, out the front door.

There was no pain as my body slammed against the cold cement outside.

Adrenaline was coursing through my veins. The feeling was in every part of my body: every finger, every toe, was alive and on fire.

"Get out of here!" I heard John yell.

Terry rushed toward where I lay on the ground, but John was able to grab him around the waist and pull him back.

Like a chess player, I strategically waited for the next move.

"It's over, man," John said.

Terry spit over his shoulder at me as his brother grabbed him by the collar to lead him back into the store.

That was all of the opening I needed.

I shot up, ran over to the window, and banged my fists against it, wildly screaming Corri's name.

This time Terry was not so forgiving. He ripped himself from John's grasp, then charged toward me. "I'll teach you to hit me, you freak!"

Terry pried one of my arms from the window, drew back, and delivered a massive blow to my face. A searing pain shot up through my nose and into my sinuses.

I stumbled back. Before I could regain my balance he delivered another swift blow to my stomach. I tried to take in a breath, but it felt as if the air had been replaced by knives.

Corri was screaming from inside the store for him to stop. Her voice gave me the strength to straighten up and I was able to catch a brief glimpse of her through the window.

"What the hell are you smiling at, freak?" Terry drew back and hit me again in the face.

This time I lost my balance completely. There was an awful crunch above my right eye and blood immediately spilled down into my face. As I fell to the ground, I instinctively curled into a ball and protected my face with my hands. Terry was able to get in a few good kicks before his brother could reach him.

"Terry, that's enough!" He tried to pull his brother up by the back of the shirt but the fabric ripped. Terry was once again on top of me.

"Stop it!" John yelled. Locking both of his arms around Terry's wide chest, it took all of John's strength to heave him off me. "I said, stop it! You're gonna kill him, Terry!"

A panting and exhilarated Terry smiled a wide toothy smile at me as he gave in to his brother's force.

John looked down at me first, surveying the damage, and then gave a nervous glance down the sidewalk. "You okay?"

The blood seeped through my fingers and streamed down the right side of my face. I was obviously not okay.

"I think you better get moving along." He stood next to Terry at the entrance to the shop, almost as if I was some rowdy kid they had just bounced from their uncle's bar. "You heard me. Go on, get moving."

A small crowd of onlookers had gathered outside—mostly business owners just opening their shops for the day. I struggled to my feet and looked around. I put one hand on my hip and raised my other hand up in the air as if to say, "Enough."

But it wasn't enough.

I flew back to the window and smacked it one more time. The palm of my hand left a red bloody print on the glass. Before John and Terry could get to me, I took off running. I ran as fast as my legs could carry me.

The blood, thick and salty in my mouth, streaked across my face as I flew. Warm tears from my eyes washed patches of the blood from my face exposing tiny rivers and valleys of bare skin.

But I wasn't crying in pain.

It was quite the opposite actually.

I was laughing.

Chapter 8

Not wanting my parents to see what had happened to my face, I left a note on my bedroom door, saying that I had gone to the library and would grab something to eat in town. I heard them come up twice during the evening and knock, but thankfully they never tried to come in.

I went to sleep quite early and was a bit surprised at how easily the dream world appeared this time, but maybe that was because I had fallen asleep with the exact image of where I wanted to go pictured perfectly in my mind.

Smoke billowed up from one of two chimneys on the little stone house. It was dusk and from outside the fire made the windows glow a warm yellowish orange. Magnificent tall pines towered in the background.

I could envision no place more inviting to come into from out of the cold. The home was just one story and made completely out of river stones of various shapes and sizes, which over time had all weathered to similar shades of grey. Three small steps made of the same stone led up to the home's old, wooden front door. A little peaked roof, covered in snow, sheltered the entryway.

As I made my way to the house fresh snow crunched under my sneakers. Little white clumps clung to the bottoms of my jeans making them wet and stiff.

There was a large bay window to the left of the front door and a smaller window on the right. A small bundle of freshly cut firewood was neatly stacked next to the steps.

The door was heavy and it creaked as I pushed it open. Immediately the smell of old newspapers and burning wood filled my senses. In a small sitting room to the left, a fire crackled away in an old stone fireplace. To the right sat a rustic wooden dining table with an old fashioned kitchen behind it.

It was perfect.

I walked over to the table and began re-positioning the two chairs that sat beneath it—moving them next to each other, apart, then back next to each other again. It seemed silly to sit so far across from one another, but then again it was also a bit odd to be side by side, wasn't it? After a few circles around the table I finally decided on one chair at the head of the table with the other chair to its right.

I wanted everything to be ready before Corrine got there. Not knowing how soon she would arrive made me move with a sense of urgency. Hurrying into the kitchen, I placed my hands on top of the stove, closed my eyes, and concentrated. I could feel the warmth spread beneath my fingers like sand on a warm summer day. When I leaned down to open the oven, a wave of heat blasted me in the face, stinging my eyes and the edges of my hairline.

The heat carried with it the smell of familiar holiday spices; thyme, rosemary, and marjoram.

Thanksgiving was a meal I looked forward to all year. If food could express an emotion, I'd always thought Thanksgiving dinner would convey love. It was warm, rich, and always served with good laughs and good company.

Centered in the oven in front of me now, cooked to a perfect golden brown, was a turkey. It was seated in a deep pan atop a bed of baby red potatoes, various vegetables, and stuffing. The pan was heavy, and you'd think by the way I teetered carefully over to the table with it that I had actually spent the many hours it should have taken to prepare such a feast.

With the food prominently displayed in the center, I moved to the head of the table and sat down. Bowing my head, I folded my hands in front of me as if in prayer.

The tip of my nose grazed my fingers as I lifted my head back up. Resting my chin on my hands, I opened my eyes and smiled. Man, I was getting good at this! The spread on the table was even better than I had envisioned.

Sterling silver platters and serving dishes ran the entire length of the table. The metal gleamed under the turkey and vegetables which were now situated on their respective platters. Mounds of red and white grapes dripped over the edges of another dish onto the table and steam was rising off a ladle of gravy in a bowl next to the turkey.

White china plates and crisp linen napkins were placed directly in front of each chair and three large floral arrangements were equally spaced across the table. They were sphere-shaped and made up of what looked to be white roses and white hydrangeas. In the spaces between were two amazing candelabras. They were also made of sterling silver, and each had one raised candle in the center flanked by two more on each side. The candles, like the flowers, napkins, and plates, were all white.

Chilling in a bucket of ice, finishing off the amazing table setting, was my first act of teenage rebellion—a bottle of champagne. Two jeweled goblets were placed directly beside it. I was about to meet a beautiful girl, in a secret place, where we had access to things we weren't supposed to. For the very first time in my life, I felt like I was included in the fun and mischief that other kids my age had been experiencing for years.

I stood up to get a pack of matches from the kitchen, but stopped. Who needed matches? I snapped my fingers and felt a surge of power as the candles lit themselves at my will. I looked over at the fire and watched the flames kick up.

Taking my place at the head of the table, I scooted the chair out a bit so that it faced the door, sat down, and waited.

ଔଓ

The first couple of times the candles melted down more than an inch, I closed my eyes and immediately built them back up, but by the third time, I let them go.

Where was she? Had I mistaken what had happened at the store? No, she had known who I was. She had known about the dreams. I could tell that from the way she looked at me. But then again, she never said anything to confirm that, did she?

Was I crazy? Did I imagine what had happened at the store? Was I imagining this?

There is something very desperate indeed about the exact moment at which the scales tip—when anticipation turns to despair.

The once roaring fire became a smoldering heap of ash. The candles, which had so recently given me a sense of power, were now nothing more than cruel reminders of how long I had been waiting.

As dawn broke outside, and the light in the room began to change, I stood and blew out the candles.

She wasn't coming.

Grabbing the champagne and one of the goblets off the table, I opened the door and went outside.

The front steps felt cold and hard under me as I took a seat. The once majestic landscape now looked stark and lonely in the early morning light. I thought of nothing as I sipped the champagne.

Snow began to fall. They were big fat flakes—so soft and light that they appeared to be coming down in slow motion. I put the goblet down on the steps next to me and turned my attention to my hands.

The tips of my fingers felt numb. At first I blamed it on the cold, but then, as I started to rub my hands together, I saw it. The index and pinky fingers of my left hand were disappearing.

My eyes narrowed. I flipped my hands over studying them with a somewhat sick intensity. I suddenly had an overwhelming desire to become nothing, to enjoy the act of becoming nothing.

In fact I was so focused that I didn't even hear Corrine until she was maybe twenty feet in front of me.

It was the sound of her steps in the snow that drew my attention. I lifted my head and looked at her expressionless. She was carrying something by her side. Corrine met my gaze, but did not smile. She didn't speak. She walked directly over to me, leaned in, and without saying a word moved the object she had been holding in front of my face.

It was a mirror.

Staring back at me from the looking glass was a face I didn't know.

My skin was smooth and my facial features were symmetrical, pleasing even. My hair was still thick and black but the unruliness of it against the clean lines of my face now gave me a somewhat edgy quality. And instead of looking like an orange atop a toothpick, my skinny neck appeared muscular and proportionate to the size of my head.

The shock of the image made my mouth fall open. It was then that I noticed how straight and even my teeth were. I ran my tongue slowly over each one, marveling at the smoothness and at how white they looked against the pink of my gum line.

Even my lips were different. They were soft and full, completely void of the usual dry cracks and painful acne bumps that usually plagued them.

As I scanned my face from top to bottom, I realized about the only thing that remained unchanged about me were my eyes. But it wasn't as if I were looking at a total stranger. The effect was more like that of looking into a fun-house mirror. It was me, but it wasn't me.

Seeing myself like this, in this perfect light, was so moving and powerful that I couldn't tear my eyes away. And as my reflection faded from the glass, I never once thought to look back up at Corrine.

I was still touching my face when I woke up.

༄༅

Everything I had ever wanted to be, everything that would make my life what it was not, things that ordinarily could not be changed, were now available to me.

I felt a sharp pain in my ribcage as I sat up. I put my hand over the spot and moved slowly to the edge of the bed. There were reddish brown streaks all over the comforter. I touched my fingers just above my right eye where Terry had hit me. The gash must have opened back up during the night. It was swollen and my eyebrow was crusted over with a thick layer of new blood. My whole body ached like I had been in a car accident, which struck me as odd, because I hadn't felt any of this pain in the dream. My image in the mirror had not reflected any injuries, either.

Wrapping the stained comforter around my shoulders, I looked around the room. It was so different from the dreams. I'd never noticed it before, but there was hardly any color. There were no pictures on the walls. No photographs in frames—only a bed, a desk, a table, and a few clothes on the floor.

The pain in my side made me suck in my breath as I got to my feet. It was the weekend and I didn't have to work, but I made a large pot of coffee anyway. Everything hurt as I moved. On any normal day I would have been much more concerned about my injuries than I was. However, this was not a normal day. When compared to what had just happened in my dream, my injuries seemed almost insignificant. No, cleaning the bedspread and putting bandages on were just going to have to wait. With my blanket still about my shoulders, I hunkered down in front of the computer for what I knew was going to be a very long day.

I was consumed with desire. Not only to keep the fantasy going, but to know more about what was happening to me. Surely someone in this world must have had a similar experience. How could I be the only one?

To my surprise, I was easily able to find hundreds of thousands of pages on the net with stories from people all over the world who had stumbled upon the ability to control their dreams. The phenomenon was call "lucid dreaming," and it was coined in the early 1900's by a Dutch psychiatrist and writer named Frederik van Eeden. Not only had lucid dreaming been researched scientifically—its existence was well established.

As for someone being able to share this experience with another person? The idea was talked about on various chat forums, but I couldn't find anything like what Corrine and I were experiencing.

Stumped, I tapped my fingers on the desk and looked out the small window past my computer screen. The similarities were too strong to ignore—lucid dreaming and "The Lucid," the fact that the man who coined the term was Dutch, just like Doctor Kelly, and the story of the cat and the statue in her office.

I turned in my chair and looked back at the nightstand. It couldn't be real. It just couldn't be. Things like this just didn't happen.

Very cautiously, I walked over to the drawer, removed the black velvet pouch, and brought it back over to my desk with me. I shook the talisman out into my hand and flipped it over to inspect the word on the back again.

DROMENCIAN

Taking a sip of coffee, I used my free hand to type the word, "dromencian," into the search engine. An alert popped up right away stating that my search had yielded zero results. Assuming I must have spelled the name wrong, I picked up the talisman and looked again. I typed the word in again, slower this time. I had only entered the first part "dromen" when I noticed what the computer was displaying for possible matches. The first result was a definition. I could see from the link that dromen was a Dutch word. The English translation of which was: dreams.

This was too weird!

I quickly opened another browser window and started searching for a foreign language translation site. When I found one, I selected the "English to Dutch" option and typed in the word again. The site confirmed for me that dromen was indeed the Dutch word for dreams, but when I typed in the full word "dromencian," again there was nothing.

Frustrated, I took my hand off the keyboard and chewed at my thumbnail.

"Za Dutch speak many different languages." I could hear Doctor Kelly say in my head. "I've never understood why Americans are so satisfied wid just speaking one."

Maybe I'm searching the wrong language?

I used the backspace button to delete the word and then changed the translation option at the top of the page to "search all languages."

To my dismay the same results popped up as before–dromen meant dreams in Dutch, and there was no translation in any language for dromencian.

At least I had the first half of the word figured out.

But what if?

I scooted my chair closer to the desk.

What if I only typed in the second half of the word?

Slowly, letter by letter, I deleted "dromencian" and replaced it with "cian."

A match popped up immediately showing that "cian" was a popular Latin suffix. I felt a kind of pressure about my head as I scrolled down to read more. The suffix meant—magician or physician.

By combining both Dutch and Latin, dromencian quite literally translated out to dream magician—or doctor of dreams.

ઝઉ

Since it was the weekend and her office was closed, I was going to have to wait until Monday to confront Doctor Kelly. Until then, I would have to work very hard to make sure everyone and everything appeared normal.

Thankfully, the blood from my face had only gotten on one side of my comforter. I flipped the comforter over so that the good side was facing up as I made my bed. Washing it would have to wait, I thought. My first order of business was going to be explaining my bruised and battered body to both of my parents. Tucking the talisman deep into the drawer of my nightstand, I covered it with papers (so that nobody would be able to find it), grabbed some fresh clothes, and headed downstairs.

My parents always left the Laundromat at eleven-o-clock sharp to come up for lunch. That didn't give me much time to work with.

As soon as I walked in the door, I dragged a dining room chair into the kitchen and set it out in front of the refrigerator. Stepping up, I got a couple of large pans out of the top-most cupboards and put them on the floor. For good measure I took out a large glass vase and laid that down as well. Leaving the cupboard doors wide open, I then tipped the chair on which I'd been standing on its side.

When I was done, I quickly got in the shower. I went to work on the bloodied areas of my face with a warm washcloth. I was in bad shape, but the baggy clothes I had brought down with me covered most of the bruising. I was just finishing up with some ointment and strategically-placed band aids when I heard my mother come in. I walked out to meet her.

She gasped when she saw me. "What happened to your face?" In an overly dramatic display, my mother grabbed my chin and turned my face up toward the light.

"Mom, it's nothing. I'm fine."

"It doesn't look fine."

Actually my face looked rather good compared to yesterday. I couldn't imagine what she would have done if she had seen me right after it happened.

She put her hands on her hips and stepped back. "What happened, Travis?"

"It's really stupid." I said.

"Try me."

I swung my hair out of my eyes and said the lines I had been rehearsing in the shower. "I wanted to make you guys lunch—" Looking down I kicked my foot against the ground as if I was embarrassed.

"Go on . . ." my mother prompted.

"I wanted to make you guys lunch," I started again. "'Cause I felt really bad about how I acted at dinner the other night and—"

"And—what?" she pressed.

I motioned to the kitchen and in a sheepish voice said, "I couldn't reach the pots on the top of the refrigerator."

My mom looked to her right and carefully took in the scene I had so artfully set out for her.

For a second I was worried she wasn't buying it, but then she began to chuckle. "Well, it looks like you definitely take after your father when it comes to the kitchen."

"Mom!" I cried, feigning indignation.

"I'm sorry." My mother covered her mouth to control her laughter. "I'm sorry, honey. Are you sure you're okay?"

"Yeah. It looks worse than it is," I lied.

She put her arm around me and gave me a good squeeze, which was excruciatingly painful due to my ribs. "That was very sweet of you to try to make us lunch," she said. "How 'bout I make us something? You look like you've had enough excitement in the kitchen for one day."

I smiled. "That would be nice."

My mom picked up the mess in the kitchen and tousled my hair before handing me a tuna sandwich. She loved the idea of being able to take care of me. We ate side by side.

I was on my best behavior at dinner, too. Dad had quite a laugh as she replayed the scene of how she had found me earlier in the day.

I'll have to admit, I was rather nervous when night came. I stayed downstairs much longer than I usually did. It took me hours to fall asleep once I actually went up to my room, but that night—and the next—the dreams returned. They were even more beautiful than before, and because of them, I discovered how to do even more fantastic things.

Things I couldn't wait to share with Corrine. But for some reason, she never joined me.

Chapter 9

Although Doctor Kelly's office didn't open until nine, I was in the parking lot by seven Monday morning. To my surprise, her car was already there when I arrived—the only one in the entire lot. It was a compact family sedan, silver in color, parked appropriately under a white sign on which Doctor Kelly's name had been printed in bright blue block letters.

As I looked from her car to the building, I noticed that there was a light on inside.

I made my way over to the front door and was a little shocked to find that the door had been propped open with a book. Picking it up, I tucked the book under my arm and slipped inside.

It was eerily quiet as I walked down the dark hallway. The door to Doctor Kelly's office was wide open, and I could hear a lot of movement coming from inside. She didn't seem to notice me standing in the doorway. Classical music played softly and cardboard boxes and newspapers were scattered all about the room. Kelly was kneeling in front of one of the bookcases wrapping up a picture frame in the pages of an old magazine.

I cleared my throat and placed the book I had found in the door down on the ground next to me. Kelly didn't flinch or jump at the sound of my voice. She didn't even look up. "You're here a little early, aren't you, Travis?" She took a clip from her shirt and used it to pin her long hair up into a bun.

"What are you doing?" I asked.

Kelly reached behind her and turned off the portable CD player on the floor. She sat back on her heels and looked up at me.

"I know dis may seem a little sudden," she said. "I was going to call all of my patients today before I left."

"You're leaving?" The question came out a little more desperate than I had intended, but in just a week's time almost everything I had ever known had been flipped upside down. This was a bit more than I could process at the moment.

She pushed aside a few of the boxes to make a spot for me on the ground next to her. "Come sit down wid me."

I stayed in the doorway, my hands defiantly balled into fists. "What's going on?" I demanded.

Doctor Kelly looked taken aback by my response. "I'm sorry, Travis. I had no idea you'd react dis way. I didn't mean I was going away forever. I just have some business to take care of somewhere else for a little while," she said. "Dat's all. I'll be coming back."

"No," I said. "That's not what I meant. What I meant was—what's going on with me?" I pulled the talisman from my pocket.

Her eyes widened.

I held it out to her. "What did you do to me?"

She looked from me to the talisman, then back to me again. "No." She shook her head. "It couldn't be."

I stood my ground.

"You mean it worked?" she gasped.

My eyes narrowed.

There was a pause, then Doctor Kelly did the strangest thing. She slapped her hands on her thighs and jumped up to meet me. "Well, isn't dat somezing!" Kelly clapped me on the back and laughed. "Isn't dat somezing! Dat's just amazing, Travis!" Her bright blue eyes sparkled. She acted like I'd just won something—like she was congratulating me.

"So it… it's real?" I stammered. "Lucid dreaming? The Lucid? It's all real?"

"Well, I zink you can answer dat better dan anyone else now, don't you?"

I was stunned. How could she be so casual about all of this?

"What are you?"

Kelly laughed again. "Whatever do you mean?"

"Are you really a doctor? Are you part of the Lucid? What are you?"

"Of course I'm a doctor! I'm one of da oldest kinds of doctors dere are!" Doctor Kelly hurried over to the bookcase and grabbed a large book from the bottom shelf. She brought it over to her desk and began flipping through pages as she continued talking. "Of course dey didn't give us credit as healers until da 1800's."

Stopping at a page about halfway through, she put her finger in the middle and turned the book to me. "Dere." Her finger was on a drawing of a woman sitting cross-legged. The woman's eyes were closed and there were various stars around her. Under the illustration it read, "Witchcraft: The Ancient Art of Magic in a Modern World."

I leaned back. "You're a witch?"

"Shhh! Please, keep your voice down." Doctor Kelly took a seat on the corner of the desk and leaned in.

"Yes. I am a doctor, Travis. But yes, I am also what I suppose you could consider a witch. A high priestess, actually."

It was hard for me to wrap my mind around what she was telling me. I just stood there blinking at her in disbelief.

"Here, look." Kelly put the book on her lap. She spoke quickly and excitedly as she flipped through the pages. "Tens of zousands of witches were killed during da Middle Ages. See?"

Doctor Kelly used her index finger to point to various pictures of women being burned at the stake; their faces twisted in torture, their accusers pointing and jeering. "Da Salem Witch Trials? I'm sure you've at least read about zose in school. Zose weren't until the 1690's, but in Holland we had a very tolerant society. Dey had already done away wid punishments for witchcraft forty years earlier."

Kelly shut the book and held it close to her chest. "Being dat my family is from Holland means we have one of da oldest bloodlines out dere, somezing which is highly regarded among odder witches."

Still skeptical, I tilted my head to the side. I took in her pretty eyes and face. "You don't look like a witch."

She giggled at that. "What? Am I supposed to have a broomstick and a pointy hat or somezing?"

I couldn't help it, but the image of Doctor Kelly on a broomstick made me smile.

Kelly put down the book and grabbed my hands. "Dere's nothing strange about being a witch," she said. "I've studied medicine all over da world. A lot of modern healing meddods and beliefs come from very old practices, so in dat sense many people could be considered witches."

"But you do like magical stuff, right?"

"Oh, I don't know how magical I am. Da magic from da talisman? Dat you did all by yourself."

I shook my head. "I don't understand. What do you mean?"

Doctor Kelly scooted closer. "Dat talisman has been in my family for a very long time, Travis. I've only ever run across a few people I even zought needed da kind of help it can offer, but dat's only part of da equation. Da talisman has to choose you. Somezing in you connected with da natural power da stone possesses. You are really somezing quite special."

I put my hand up to stop her. "Wait. So you choose people to be in the Lucid?"

Kelly could tell she was getting ahead of herself. "Of course, I'm so sorry. Yes. I am one of what we call da 'keepers' of da secret of da Lucid. It was an honor bestowed on me and now it is an honor dat has been bestowed on you."

"But you said it could help me."

Kelly crossed her arms and leaned back. "You can experience zings you ordinarily wouldn't zink possible in dreams, but da similarities between waking life and dreams are really quite great."

I stared at her blankly.

Kelly cleared her throat and patiently tried again. "By opening yourself up and exploring da dream state, you are able to unlock your true potential. Dat's what dis world is all about. It is a learning ground. Da talisman was created for da sole purpose of preserving ancient societies—like mine. When all seemed lost, someone would be chosen to find da inspiration and greatness needed to lead deir people out of da darkest of times."

"What about all the people I found online, that do this? Are they part of the Lucid, too?"

"Hmmmm," Kelly hummed. "It's hard to explain dis. You are right, lucid dreaming is not just for members of our world. It's a hard zing to learn how to do, but for da people dat figure it out, yes, dey can get da same kind of benefit out of it. Our world is more of a world widdin deir world, if dat makes sense. Da real difference between us and zem is dat our connection with one another is much stronger and much more—" Kelly stopped.

"More what?"

"Permanent." Doctor Kelly's eyes narrowed and her voice took on a somber tone. "You are da new keeper of da secret of da Lucid, Travis. It is a secret you must guard wid your life. No one can ever know about us. If anyone outside of da circle finds out, it could endanger what we have worked centuries to create."

I immediately thought of Corrine. "I—" I stopped. I wanted to tell Doctor Kelly.

"You what, Travis?"

—but the best part about the dreams was Corrine. What if Kelly could stop her from being there?

"I–can do that." I agreed.

Corrine hadn't been in my dreams for a couple of nights. Maybe it was a fluke? Maybe she couldn't even get in anymore.

Kelly nodded in approval. Then she looked down at my hand where the talisman lay pressed in my fist. "Let me see it," she said.

I unfurled my fingers.

Kelly brushed her hand over it. "Talismans are amazing zings," she cooed. "Dey have da power to make all human desires, hopes, and expectations come true."

That was it! I thought. That's why I was handsome in the dreams. If the talisman had something to do with human desires, of course my appearance would be altered. Corrine would never want to be with someone like me. She would never desire someone like me. That must be the reason I looked different in the dreams.

Doctor Kelly hopped off the desk. "Now, when I come back we'll have lots of time to talk, but right now I'm going to need you to be very careful about all of dis."

I had forgotten she was leaving. "No! Wait!" I cried. "You can't leave. Not now!"

"I'm afraid I don't have a choice," she said. "I have to go to Holland to—"

"Holland? You're going to Holland?" That was halfway across the world!

I could feel myself losing my breath. "What am I supposed to do while you're gone? What if something happens?"

Doctor Kelly put her arm around me. "Calm down, Travis. Everyzing is going to be just fine. I'm setting up arrangements for a sort of holiday among my people—dat's all."

She began ushering me towards the door. "I'll be back in a couple of weeks. All you have to do until zen is enjoy da dreams. Learn more about what you can do. But be careful," Doctor Kelly warned. "Da talisman is very important. Don't break it, and for goodness sakes, don't lose it. Never let it out of your sight."

Kelly kept moving until we reached the front door to the office building. She put her hands on my shoulders and turned to face me. "It'll be okay," she said. "It was scary for all of us at first, but I will teach you everyzing you need to know, in due time—and believe me, dere's a lot to learn. Now that I know you're dere—if anyzing happens? If you need help? I'll know. Do you understand?"

I didn't, but I nodded.

"I do have ways of contacting you if I need to." She opened the door and led me out.

I stood on the sidewalk completely dazed—not yet fully able to process what all had just happened.

Doctor Kelly surveyed the parking lot. "I'm sorry to rush you out," she said. "It doesn't look very good to have a teenage boy in my office wid me during off hours—not to mention a patient."

I nodded. Again.

"We'll talk more about dis when I get back. Okay? And like I said—I do have ways of contacting you, if you need it."

Mistaking my state of shock for quiet acceptance, Kelly seemed satisfied with my reaction. "You have received an amazing gift, Travis. Treat it as such."

I murmured an odd kind of "thank-you" and "I will," before stumbling around to go.

As I walked away, Doctor Kelly called out one more time to me, "Be careful, Travis, and remember— Don't. Tell. Anyone."

It was a promise I was going to keep for all of five minutes.

Chapter 10

There was a pay phone at the gas station directly across the street from Doctor Kelly's office. I balanced the chained phone book on my knee. Pressing the receiver to my ear, I silently praised my mother, who had always drilled into my head the need to carry spare change.

"Hello?"

Her voice released hundreds of butterflies in my stomach. "Corrine? It's me. Travis."

There was a pause. "Hold on a second."

There was a shuffling noise followed by muffled voices. I could make out Corrine telling Marissa that she needed to take the call in the other room. There was some more muffled speech and shuffling before she finally got back on the line. "What are you doing calling me here?" Corrine asked in a hushed tone.

"Where have you been?"

She was silent for a moment then said, "I've been sleeping during the day."

It stung.

The phone book fell off my knee and I tripped into the side of the booth.

"Travis? Are you there?"

Never once over the past couple of nights had I thought her absence could have been the result of a purposeful decision. I faltered a bit before continuing.

"I know what's going on, Corrine. There's this doctor. I see this doctor now and then. That's not the point though. She gave me something. It's making me—or making us I should say, have these things; dreams. They're making us have dreams. They're called lucid dreams."

"I know what lucid dreams are," she said, cutting me off. Her tone was cold. "I do have a computer, you know. Don't you think I looked?"

Marissa's voice boomed in the background.

"Hang on a sec," Corrine yelled. "I'll be out in a minute!"

"Look, Travis, I have to go. I don't know what you want me to do here."

"Meet me somewhere." I said.

One week ago I would had laughed if someone told me I was going to ask Corrine Johnson to meet me somewhere and I would have downright fallen on the floor if I was told she was going to accept.

ʚϾ

Corrine started taking off her apron the moment she saw me pass by the window. We had agreed to meet in the alley just down from her work–right behind John and Terry's bar.

My conversation with her had been so brief, and we were both so rattled with nerves, that the dangerous nature of the location hadn't occurred to either of us.

I sucked in my breath as I crossed in front of the bar. The window was dark which gave me a small sense of relief, but just as I was about to turn the corner of the building, I heard Terry call out to me.

"Hey, Hunchback!"

His voice sent shivers up my spine.

"Yeah, I'm talking to you. Marissa told me that's what they call you at school." Terry leaned his back against the frame of the open doorway and casually lit a cigarette.

"I thought we told you not to come back here."

I stood frozen at the entrance to the alley, not wanting to look at him.

"You got balls, I'll give ya that," he said. "I gave ya a pretty good ass kickin'." Terry flipped his lighter closed,

I felt myself flinch.

"I mean, I get it, she's hot," he said, taking a drag off his cigarette. "But come on, it's not like she's ever gonna go for someone like you."

There was nothing I could do, I was completely outmatched–I knew that; even so, I felt a small fire ignite in the pit of my stomach.

"Let's say she did go for you–not that that's ever gonna happen, but for shits and giggles let's just say that she did. Would you even know what to do with her? Have you ever touched a girl?" Terry's voice became muted as he continued to berate me.

It was like I was drowning inside of myself and his voice was a chain pulling me deeper into the abyss. If I could just get my body to work, I thought. If only I knew how to swim.

Terry lifted his fingers to his face. "Know what this is?" he asked. He formed the shape of a "v" in front of his mouth and made a few grotesque movements with his tongue. "What if she—"

"Who are you talking to out here?" John's voice came booming from behind.

Terry jumped and spun around to face his brother inside.

The sheer terror of the two of them standing together was enough to slam me back into my body; and in the split second it took for Terry to turn around, I was able to make my escape.

"Jesus, Terry. Haven't you done enough? Leave the poor kid alone!" I heard John yell as I flew around the corner. "Put that thing out and get back in here. We've got shit to do."

I ran until I got about halfway down the alley. Then I stopped and flattened myself against the wall. The passageway was narrow, but not very long– and thankfully, it let out onto a safe residential street. If he came after me, if given a head start, I thought I could make it.

As if in synch with my inner monologue, footsteps thundered into the alley behind me. My head jerked up, and my legs tensed, ready for the race.

"Travis?"

Corrine stopped running as soon as she saw me. She gave me a weak little wave before hurrying over.

"Hi."

She looked nervously over her shoulder then gushed, "I'm so sorry. I'm so stupid. I forgot all about John and Terry."

I leaned to the side and looked past her at the entrance to the alleyway. "Did they say anything to you?"

"Terry was outside. He gave me a really weird look, but no, he didn't say anything. Why?" she asked. "Did he say something to you?"

The fire in my stomach began to die down, but there was a shakiness in my voice that I prayed wouldn't betray me. "Nah. Didn't see him."

We both tried to say something next, but did so at the same time and stepped on each other's words.

"I'm sorry," I said. "I'm not very good at this."

"No. Go ahead. You go first." Corrine wore a thin cardigan over her usual t-shirt and jeans and she hugged it tightly around her body. She was trying to look anywhere but at me. I hoped it was because she was nervous, but it hurt.

"I know what's going on," I told her.

Corrine took a firm stance, hugged her sweater closer, and nodded for me to begin.

I got right to it. She listened patiently and did not say a word as I recounted in great detail everything that had happened with Doctor Kelly. I told her about how I had gotten the talisman, what I found on the Internet, and about the bizarre and brief meeting I had just had with Doctor Kelly.

She stared at her feet the whole time I talked.

When I was finished I asked, "Corrine? You believe me, right?"

She looked up and stared off to the side. "No? Yeah? I don't know."

She used the palm of her hand to wipe at her eyes. "What choice do I have? It's either that or I'm crazy, right? I just don't know what you want me to do, here. I didn't ask for any of this, you know."

She sounded resentful, and her not wanting to look at me was starting to make me angry, which was probably the reason I did what I did next.

"Go out with me," I said.

"What?"

"Go out with me tonight."

It didn't come out at all like a question.

"You mean, like in the dreams?" The uneasiness in her voice only made me more direct.

"No. I mean like dinner. Somewhere in town. I hear people do stuff like that, you know. Go out and eat? It's not exactly a new idea."

Corrine bit at the nail on her middle finger.

"Travis—"

"Look, I live right around the corner," I interrupted, pointing in the direction of my house. "When you get off work, come by, and we'll go out. That is, unless you have something more interesting to do."

I paused and then added with sarcasm—"More interesting than meeting up with someone you're possibly having a first-of-its-kind paranormal experience with, that is."

Corrine looked at me for the first time. "No," she said.

"No, you don't want to meet up?"

"No, I don't have anything more interesting to do . . ." her words trailed off at the end. She smiled at me, and for the first time in the real world, I felt the stirrings of the comfortable bond we had created in the dreams.

A bond that was broken almost as soon as it had started.

"Oh, shoot! What time is it?" Corrine checked an imaginary watch on her wrist and started walking back toward the entrance to the alley. "I'm so sorry. I really have to get back. The register's acting up again and we've been super busy this morning. I told Marissa I just needed to run some change over to my mom for the parking meter."

I hurried after her. "What time do you get off work?"

"Sometime around seven."

Right before we hit the street, I pulled Corrine back by her hand. "I live just above the Laundromat," I said.

She looked down at my hand.

I quickly snatched it away. "Just so you know," I tried to finish, embarrassed.

"I know where you live," she said.

I crinkled my eyebrows.

"You are like the only person in the whole world still listed in the phone book, you know."

She had looked me up?

"So? What?" she asked. "Do I just ring the bell to the laundromat?"

If she came to the front door, I knew my parents would never let me hear the end of it.

I tried to act nonchalant, but I have to admit I felt my chest expand as I answered, "Nah. You can just come on up. I have my own apartment."

Her eyes widened with surprise. "Really?"

"Well, kind of."

Corrine had been right—great things *were* great for impressing other people. I'd never felt one ounce of pride over having my own apartment until that very moment.

"There's a stairwell on the right side of the building," I instructed. "You'll see it from the street. I'll leave the door unlocked for you. Just go all the way up the stairs. I'm the only room on the top floor."

"Cool."

Just as we stepped forward to exit the alley, where she would be taking a left and I would be taking a right, Corrine spun back around to face me. As she did, a strange dark shadow of movement behind her snagged the corner of my vision.

"So, I'll see ya tonight," she said.

The idea of her coming over quickly overrode all else and an explanation for the movement behind her was never able to fully formulate.

"Yeah. See ya tonight," I confirmed.

"Okay."

"Okay." It sounded more like a business arrangement than a date and I put my hand out to shake hers. Corrine looked down at my hand and laughed. I pulled back, mortified, but she reached out and grabbed it anyway. She gave my hand a quick, light shake and then let go.

"I'll see you tonight, Travis." Corrine jogged backwards a few steps and gave me a little wave before turning around and taking off in a sprint toward the coffee shop.

"See you at seven!" I called out.

She shot her hand up in the air to let me know she'd heard me.

Not that I thought she needed the reminder. I just wanted to hear it out loud again.

Chapter 11

That evening, I rushed through dinner as fast as I could. My parents were thrilled when I told them I needed some cleaning supplies to take up to my room.

"You're cleaning?" my mom exclaimed. "I never thought I'd see the day when you'd clean without being asked."

Still chewing, my dad picked up his fork and pointed it toward my mom. "I told you that apartment was a good idea," he said. "Independence breeds responsibility."

"You were right, dear. You were right."

I was rummaging under the kitchen sink to get what I needed as my dad called out, "Keep this up young man, and maybe we'll start talking about getting you a car."

"Now I don't know if we need to go that far," my Mom interjected. "Do you know how much a car costs these days?"

With my arms full of cleaners and paper towels I hurried to the front door. "Gotta go!" I said.

Thinking better of it, I ran back to my mother and gave her a quick peck on the cheek before heading out. "I'll bring these back down tomorrow, Mom."

I'm sure they thought my haste was in response to the car comment. They were both too busy congratulating themselves to ask.

ಬಿಓ

As promised, Corrine arrived just a few minutes after seven. I had picked up my room to the best of my ability and it was a good thing I did, because as soon as I opened the door, she walked right past me into the main living area.

"Come on in," I joked to the empty doorway. I took a quick look down the hallway and then locked the door behind us.

"Oh, sorry," she said quietly. Corrine was wearing the same thin cardigan she had had on earlier in the day and in her hand was a large paper sack. She took the sweater off and placed it on the floor next to her along with the bag. There wasn't much to look at and I'm sure my blank walls were quite different than what surrounded her at home.

"It's pretty cool your parents gave you your own place," she said, turning around in a big slow circle.

"Yeah, it's all right, I guess."

She gave me a knowing smile as she walked over to the window by my desk. "They don't know I'm here, do they?"

I shook my head.

"Didn't think so."

She peered out the blinds, then turned around to inspect the few books I had sitting by my computer. Placing her index finger on each one, she stopped when she got to the book I had bought at her store the week before. The night the dreams began.

"Oh my gosh," she gasped. "I forgot." She clutched the book to her chest. "That was you." She hung her head. "Terry was being so stupid that day. I really should have done something."

I suddenly felt embarrassed. Walking over to her, I took the book out of her hands and put it back on the desk. "We should probably get going." I said, motioning towards the door. "It's dark out and you're probably pretty hungry by now, right?"

"Actually…I thought we could eat here." Corrine went over to the bag she had brought. She picked it up off the floor and looked inside. "I brought some stuff from the store. I didn't know what you'd like, so I took a little bit of everything—some scones, some bagels, and a couple of muffins. It's not really dinner stuff, but it's pretty good. If you have some coffee or tea or something that would be…"

Corrine stopped when she saw how I was looking at her.

"So, you don't want to go out in public with me. Is that it?"

Corrine's face flushed and she stammered a bit before trying to recover. "No, that's not what I'm saying at all."

"I'm ugly, not stupid," I said, turning to the dinette table in the corner of the room.

Corrine followed close on my heels. "Travis, wait."

I bent down and jammed the plug of the coffee maker into the wall.

Corrine put the bag on the table. Then, she leaned down and put a hand on my shoulder. "Please. That's not what I meant."

"What? You wanted me to make coffee," I muttered. "So that's what I'm doing."

Corrine reached in front of me and pulled the plug out of the wall. "Travis, this isn't about you. What we're getting together to talk about isn't exactly an appropriate conversation to be having in public. What if someone hears us?"

"No, what if someone sees us. That's what you're really thinking. We're bound to run into at least one person we know, aren't we? What would you say? What would they think?"

"Stop it!" she yelled. "Stop putting words in my mouth!"

"Shh," I hissed, pointing to the floor below us. "My parents will hear." I didn't want to argue with her, but Corrine wasn't acting at all like she did in the dreams. She was so much softer in the dreams. Her voice never had the kind of edge to it that it had now. Was it all an act? Was she only nice to me in the dreams because I looked different? I was starting to think maybe Corrine wasn't the person I'd thought she was.

"You're not perfect," I said in a raised whisper. "So stop acting like this is all about you being nice and considerate."

"Why are you attacking me?" she whispered back.

"LOOK at me!" I stood up and dropped my arms down by my side in defeat. "Just look at me. You haven't looked at me for more than two seconds since you found out who I was."

Corrine didn't take the bait. "Don't give me an act!" she fired back. "I never said I was perfect. A week ago, I didn't even know who you were. Now you come to me and say that some doctor gave you a magic necklace and we're stuck in some sort of dream world together? What the hell? Do you know how crazy that sounds? What do you expect me to do? Be your girlfriend? I don't even know you!"

"That didn't stop you from kissing me in the dreams—when you thought I was someone else."

"It was a dream, Travis. People do things in dreams they don't do in real life!"

"So what you're saying is you wouldn't kiss me in real life."

"This is ridiculous." Corrine threw her hands up in the air. "I'm fighting with a complete stranger over things I've done in my dreams."

She stomped over to the middle of the room and grabbed her cardigan up off the floor. "I should just go," she said.

"Maybe you should."

"Fine."

"Fine," I agreed. "Go! It's not gonna change what's happening. You can't keep sleeping during the day."

"Oh, yeah?" Corrine threw her sweater fiercely over her shoulders. "Watch me!"

With that she marched over to the door, undid the lock, and stormed out.

It was silent. I felt a buzzing in my face and a wave of panic washed over me. I didn't want her to go. What was I doing?! Why was I ruining this?

I ran into the stairwell after her.

"Corrine! Wait!" I screamed from the top of the stairs, but she was already at the bottom.

"Damn it!"

Leaving the door to my room wide open, I flew down the stairwell and tore out of the door after her. She was walking fast and by running I was able to catch up with her fairly quickly on the street.

"Corrine!" I grabbed her by the arm as I yelled her name.

She whipped around to face me—her face full of anger.

I backed off a bit and lowered my voice. "Please," I said. "Don't go. I put my hands up, palms out. "I'm sorry."

Then I said it again. "I'm sorry."

Corrine looked from my hands to me.

I gave her a pained grin and shrugged my shoulders. Had I just blown everything? I really liked this girl, but I didn't know how to act with her outside of the dreams. In the dreams, I could change the things I didn't like about myself. Here, I was just plain-old, awkward Travis. I couldn't seem to do anything right.

Corrine took in a deep breath and paused before letting it all out in one big frustrated groan. In that moment, I could tell she was just as lost as I was. The rules on this plane were far different than on whatever the plane of existence was where we had actually met and gotten to know each other. If we were going to have any hope of figuring the dreams out, we were somehow going to have to find a way to work together here in the real world.

Her shoulders slumped. Corrine looked at me—she really looked at me this time. Her expression softened as she gently reached out to touch the swollen area above my eye. "That looks terrible," she said. "Does it hurt?"

I looked down at my feet. "It'll be all right."

Corrine pulled her hand back from my face and sidled up next to me. She weaved her arm inside my own. "Come on," she said softly.

Corrine started walking, but I stayed firmly rooted to the spot.

"Come on," she said again.

"Where are we going?"

"You said you wanted to go out, right? Well, we're going out." She smiled. "Sort of."

"Where?"

"Let's just say I know this terrific little place where we can go get some coffee and nobody can hear what we're talking about."

With her free hand Corrine lifted the keys to the store out of her pocket and rattled them in the air in front of us.

"You really want to do this?" I asked.

"You're right, you know. I can't keep sleeping during the day. Call me crazy, but I don't think there's much of a need in this town for an all-night coffee house."

Corrine and I looked at the businesses around us. It wasn't even eight o'clock yet and the streets were almost completely empty.

"I see what you mean."

Corrine gave me a light punch to the arm. She tugged at me again and this time I followed.

Arm in arm we began our stroll to the coffee house. All was quiet until we crossed the alley where we had met earlier in the day.

"Nice night for a stroll, isn't it?"

A dark figure emerged from the shadows. Corrine and I froze as Terry pulled down the hood of his black sweatshirt, revealing his face.

"Terry, we were just …"

Corrine fumbled for the right words to say.

"Nah, no need to explain," he said in a jovial way. "Nice to see you two kids together."

His tone was friendly, but there was something so unnatural about it that it frightened me far more than if he had come out screaming at us.

To her credit, Corrine didn't let go of my arm.

"No, really, I think it's great," he said.

Terry looked from Corrine to me.

Unable to hold his gaze, I shifted my eyes from his to the ground.

"Hey, look. I'm really sorry about earlier." Terry made a whistling sound as he twirled his finger up in the air. "I just get in these moods sometimes. We're guys. You know how it is."

I nodded absentmindedly, not taking my eyes off the ground.

Terry looked back and forth between us one more time and smiled. "Well," he said smacking his lips and inhaling deeply through his nose. "Have a nice night. Think I'm gonna take a little walk myself."

He pulled his hood up over his head and took off whistling in the direction we had just come from.

"Try not to get into too much trouble," he called out cheerfully.

Corrine looked over her shoulder at him and then back at me with surprise. "That was weird."

Chapter 12

We sat on a blanket behind the counter. Corrine looked me right in the eye as she handed me a cup of coffee and took a seat on the floor next to me.

She did a good job of trying to make me feel like my appearance wasn't bothering her.

Of course, she had kept the lights off so no one could see us from outside, but the moonlight coming through the windows illuminated the store just enough so that once our eyes adjusted, we were able to see each other quite well.

"So, it's pretty cool isn't it?" she asked.

"What's that?"

"The dreams, silly. What else would we be talking about?" Corrine cradled an oversized ceramic mug in both hands. It had a picture of a moose on it.

"Yeah, I'm still not even sure I believe it."

"There's something I don't get, though," she said. "I spent the entire weekend reading just about everything that's ever been written on lucid dreaming. And, as far as I can tell, it's not supposed to involve other people. Not like it is with us anyway."

"Maybe we share the same dream."

Corrine paused. "I like that." She took a sip of her coffee and smiled sweetly at me. "I meant what I said in the dreams, ya know. You're not like other guys I've met."

"And I meant everything I said in the dreams, too."

There was an uncomfortable silence as I knew we were both replaying in our minds what some of those admissions were.

Corrine sipped nervously at her coffee, looking for the most appropriate way to brush over the topic. "It was just nice being able to be ourselves, ya know? No fears, no consequences, no regrets. It's such a significant word, isn't it?"

"What word?"

"Lucid. It means to have a clear perception of things. Don't you think it's funny that it would take a dream for us to see clearly?"

Corrine placed her coffee on the ground next to her. "Like you," she said. "Who would've known you were like this?"

"Like what?"

"Well for one, you talk!" She laughed. "I must've seen you dozens of times before. Why don't you ever say anything to anyone?"

"I've been around enough people to know what they're thinking when they stare at me. It doesn't help me any to hear them say it."

Corrine reached a hand forward and touched my knee. "I'm not gonna lie," she said. "You do look a little different. You know what though? I don't even notice it that much now that I'm talking to you."

I looked down at her hand.

She pulled it back. "You should talk more," she said, nodding. "Some people might surprise you. Not all of them…but some."

Corrine looked around the store then cleared her throat. "So what are your folks like?" she asked. "Are they cool?"

"Yeah, I guess," I said, shaking my hair out of my eyes. "They're a little too into the laundromat sometimes. They kinda act like they don't need to be around me. Like I'm already grown up and they're totally done being parents."

"Really? They're done? So how'd they do?"

"According to them? Great."

Corrine laughed. She laughed with her whole body.

It made me feel really good to be able to make her laugh like that.

"Well you're lucky," she said. "Mine are way too into me. Probably because they can't stand talking to each other anymore."

Suddenly her future dreams of having a happy little family life didn't seem so silly or ordinary to me anymore.

Corrine smiled wistfully and leaned her head to the side. "So what was your favorite part?" she asked. "In the dreams."

"You wouldn't believe me."

"Try me."

"This," I said back to her. "I've never talked to anyone like this before."

Corrine grinned. "Me neither."

"What about Marissa?"

"What about her?"

"Isn't that why you work here? I thought you two were best friends."

"Marissa?" Corrine laughed. "She's a nice girl and all, but we hardly have anything in common."

"What about John and Terry?"

Corrine raised her eyebrows. "Please, they don't even like themselves."

"I hate how he whistles," I said.

"Who? Terry? Yeah, I guess he's always done that."

"What song is it?"

"Hell if I know. I'd like to say that it's some kind of nervous habit or something, but I don't think he has any nerves—" Corrine abruptly stopped. She straightened up and made a face as if trying to figure out how to best say what she was thinking. "Don't take this the wrong way, okay?"

I nodded for her to continue.

"You kinda act like you think everyone else is happy. Like everyone's part of some big circle and you're not. Like you're missing out on it because you're a little different, but I think the truth is—"

She took a breath. "The truth is—It's not easy for anyone to connect."

I stared at her; processing the remark. It may have been a bit of a dig at my character, but damn it if it wasn't the most comforting thing I think anyone had ever said to me.

"You ever notice the best way to form a friendship with someone is to talk badly about someone else?" Corrine continued. "We all have this intense desire to put others down. Like maybe we'll all feel we belong a little bit more if everyone else doesn't."

"I think that's why I liked the dreams so much." she continued after a beat. "We didn't need any of that. We just got to be ourselves, have fun, and just … be us."

I smiled the same smile she had given me earlier and echoed what she had said before. "I like that."

We talked for hours, me and Corrine. I was shocked to discover how much we had in common. I learned, like me, she was an only child. She had dreams of seeing the world, but the farthest she had ever gotten was the next state over.

I told her about the incredible new things I had discovered how to do in the dreams, and she seemed genuinely excited to try them. She said maybe the dreams would be able to bring her fantasies of travel to life.

And even though we didn't know if she'd be able to join me again, we both agreed—that night, we were sure going to try.

કଓ

When I got home from the coffee shop, I was riddled with excitement. Bounding up the stairs, I wondered how I was ever going to be able to get to sleep.

But my excitement stalled as soon as I opened the door to my room. That's strange. Keeping my hand on the doorknob, I flashed back to my fight with Corrine earlier in the evening and how I had flown down the stairwell into the street after her. Hadn't I left the door open?

Closing it cautiously behind me, I looked around at my room. Besides the door, nothing else seemed to be out of the ordinary.

Maybe my mom had come up. It was a plausible explanation, but even as I thought it, something far worse nagged at the back of my mind.

As I scanned the room for clues, my eyes stopped when they came to the nightstand next to my bed. Even from the doorway, I could tell the drawer had been opened. I had kept it tightly shut, but there was now about an inch of space between the drawer and the stand.

A sense of dread filled my belly. Hurrying over, I ripped open the drawer and tore out all of the papers that I had so carefully arranged over the talisman. When I got to the bottom of the pile, I let out a huge sigh of relief. The black velvet pouch was still right there at the bottom.

"How silly," I thought as I reached down to pick it up. "That I could have even started to believe—" But my relief was short-lived. As my hand closed around the bag, I froze. Why was it so light?

"Oh, no. No, no, no, no, NO!" My heart immediately jumped into my throat, constricting my airways like a snake wrapped around my neck. Why was the bag so light?! And as I loosened the drawstrings and looked inside, the worst of my fears were realized. The talisman was gone.

"Where is it?!" I cried out loud to the empty room—although I already knew the answer. I had known it all along. I just hadn't wanted to see it.

In one last desperate attempt to keep the truth at bay, I yanked the drawer out of the nightstand and frantically moved my hand over every surface to see if it had somehow fallen out or behind something.

After coming up with nothing, I stumbled back onto my bed, sat down, and cradled my head in my hands. The room was spinning.

To keep myself from passing out, I sank my body down between my knees, but as I did, I was suddenly assaulted with a barrage of images and events, all strung together in a perfect storyline. My mind was finally allowing me to accept and piece together what I had been so good at pushing away.

I saw the flutter of movement outside the alley when I had first told Corrine about the talisman; and remembered the way Terry had acted when he had passed us on our way to the coffee shop earlier—almost like he had been sitting there waiting for us. How else would he have known we'd be going out together, unless he had been listening to us in the alley?

Even the black hooded sweatshirt Terry was wearing now struck me as odd—although cooler than normal for this time of year, the temperature outside certainly didn't warrant such heavy clothing. And the direction he had been walking when he passed us; he had been walking right back…

"Here." My voice cracked from the dryness in my mouth as I finished the thought.

How could I have been so stupid?

In one conversation with Corrine, not only had I spilled the entire story of the Lucid, I had also given explicit directions on how to gain entry to my apartment unnoticed. The only way I could have made it any easier would be if I had handed him a handwritten invitation!

Calligraphy would have been a very nice touch, I thought miserably.

The worst part? I knew it was Terry! I didn't think he'd go as far as breaking into my home, but I knew it had been him the moment Corrine and I had left the alley. I was just too weak, awkward, and scared of him to take a stand. What would have been the point? Why acknowledge something I could do absolutely nothing about?

Then of course there had been Corrine. "The idea of her coming to my house?" I thought. "To see me? Well, I would have done anything not to have ruined that."

I felt sick. Was she in danger now? Could Terry be waiting there in the dreams for her? Should I tell her? Should I tell Doctor Kelly?

"Oh, Doctor Kelly!" I moaned. How was I going to explain this to her? Between losing the talisman and sharing the secret with Corrine, I had already broken every single cardinal rule Kelly had laid out for me.

Groaning, I heaved myself up and rubbed the back of my head with my hand.

I was in deep.

I knew what I should do. I should tell everyone the truth right away; go back to my normal little life and forget any of this ever happened–but how could I? Telling the truth could ruin everything! Thinking Terry could show up in the dreams might scare Corrine off. And if I told Doctor Kelly about letting two people into the dreams? Well, I didn't know what she'd do, but I sure wasn't in any kind of hurry to find out. I needed some time to think. There had to be a way to fix what I'd done before anybody found out.

"Would it really be so bad if I kept this a secret?" I thought. "What if Corrine and Doctor Kelly never find out? Doctor Kelly had said herself that I was special–that the talisman didn't work for everyone. It probably couldn't even work for Terry. Besides, shouldn't I at least wait to see if he can even get into the dreams before telling anyone?"

This is how I began to rationalize my actions. It worked well too. The more questions I asked, the better I felt.

And what if Terry did show up in the dreams? He couldn't hurt us. He didn't even know how the dreams worked! I had power there that he didn't. Surely, I could protect Corrine and myself in the dreams if I had to. Heck, I could probably just wish him away!

Denial fit the situation like a glove. I felt a dangerous new confidence settle over me as I kicked off my shoes.

Kelly won't be back for a couple of weeks, right? And as she herself had said, "All you have to do until den is enjoy da dreams."

I wasn't being myself. This was not the way I would normally think, but I had never had so much to lose. For the first time in my life, I had a life. More than that, I had Corrine Johnson. She wanted to spend time with me. I didn't want to do anything that could disrupt that.

"I could fix this." I thought. If given the time, I could make everything right—starting with Corrine. I had to make sure she was safe. I didn't have the talisman, but that didn't mean my connection to it was gone. And I had gotten rather used to the routine sensations that came with getting into the lucid state. I could do this—and I had to do it now before Corrine fell asleep. In order to protect her, I needed to make sure I got to the dream first.

Sliding under the covers, I flashed back to the coffee house where Corrine and I had come up with our plan for the evening.

It wasn't much, but when we left the shop we had both agreed we would go directly home and go to sleep. We promised to set our alarm clocks so that we'd wake up at the same time and traded phone numbers so that we could call and compare notes in the morning if indeed something did happen.

With everything that had gone wrong since that conversation, I wondered just how far we were going to stray off of our intended course for the evening.

But surprisingly, as I drifted off, everything went according to plan—everything except that it was not Corrine who was waiting for me when I arrived.

Chapter 13

There were cars everywhere—rows and rows of abandoned vehicles. Rusted out junkers and the skeletal remains of what could have once been considered luxury vehicles. They stretched out as far as the eye could see in every direction from where I stood.

It was dusty and hot and I wondered why Corrine would have chosen to meet in a salvage yard. I had been thinking about the pyramids myself.

My voice hung heavy and flat in the air as I called out her name. There was no answer.

I walked over to the car nearest me. All of its windows were missing. It was an old Buick Skylark, and although the paint was obviously faded, the pale blue was most likely not too far off from the original color. I stuck my head in and looked towards the back seat.

Just as I did, there was a knocking sound on the hood. Three sharp raps. I jumped up and hit my head on the top of the door frame. Laughing with embarrassment, I rubbed at the spot with my hand as I stood up.

My laughter was immediately silenced when I saw who was standing toward the front of the car.

"Hello, Travis."

It was as if the ability to speak had suddenly been taken away from me.

"What? Not who you expected?" she asked.

Leaning against the front of the car was Doctor Kelly. "Dis was da car dat my husband first kissed me in."

She put her hand on her hip and rested her other hand down on the hood. "Or at least what I imagine it would look like now. It's funny da zings dat you remember da most."

I blinked hard a few times, trying to readjust the image, but she was still there. "I told you I had ways of checking up on you," she said. "And if you're trying to figure out wedder or not you're dreaming I'm here? Well, dat would be radder counter-productive. Don't you zink?"

"What *are* you doing here?"

She straightened up and walked over to me. "We need to talk, Travis."

Kelly turned sideways and waved her hand in front of her. As she did, a sort of vortex opened. "Walk wid me."

I looked up at the tunnel. It seemed as though it were made of some sort of smoke or liquid. You could still see the cars and the lot through it, but it was like she had stopped the dream and somehow pushed all of the images off to the side, like it was a little sliver of frozen time in our thoughts.

"It's safe," Kelly said flippantly.

I watched with amazement as she entered the tunnel. When I realized she wasn't going to wait for me, I hurried after.

As I caught up with her, she asked, "Do you like it here?"

I was staring hard, still trying to determine if she was real, but she didn't look back at me. Her gaze was fixed on a point far ahead of us.

"Who wouldn't?" I answered.

She raised her eyebrows. "Well I'm glad dat da two of you are having such a good time in our little world."

I practically choked on my own tongue. She knew about Corrine! And if she knew about her, what else did she know about?

"I was—I was going to tell you!" I pleaded. "I was! I swear! I didn't know if it was real or not. I just wanted to be sure before—"

Kelly stopped walking and raised her hand to quiet me. "What's done is done," she said. "Where is da talisman?"

The blood drained from my face and I felt my knees go weak. Losing the talisman was surely a far worse offense than just dreaming about a girl I had a crush on.

"Where is it, Travis? Tell me—does she have da talisman, or do you have it?"

The question caught me off guard. I stared back at her blankly and wondered why she was asking about Corrine.

"Dere's no need to be coy wid me. You're bod in dis world, so dat means you must have shared it wid her."

"But I thought you—" Not wanting to implicate myself, I stopped. Did this mean she didn't know about Terry?

"Speak up, Travis. Does she have da talisman or not?"

"No …?" My voice was unsteady and my answer came out sounding more like a question.

"So you do have it?"

Shaking my head, the confusion read across my face like a bright, flashing, neon sign. Being careful to avoid the Terry situation, I still answered the question as truthfully as I could.

"Corrine's never even seen the talisman."

She said nothing, but gave me a long hard stare. Doctor Kelly was pretty good at reading people—it was her job, after all. And I could feel myself start to tremble ever so slightly as she silently scrutinized my facial expressions, my tone, even my body language.

When she was done, Kelly let out a deep breath and raised her eyebrows.

"Isn't dat somezing," she whispered to herself.

"What? What's something?"

Kelly turned back to me. "Dis poses an entirely different problem," she said. "We have a lot to talk about, young man. But don't zink dis means dat you are off da hook," she added. "You still should have told me about dis."

I nodded, somewhat relieved that she knew about Corrine, but totally overjoyed that she didn't seem to know anything about Terry yet. In fact, I'd expected her to be much more upset over Corrine than she was. For a brief moment, I considered telling her about Terry, but I stopped myself. I didn't want to press my luck. Even though Terry had stolen the talisman, it was still gone—and it had been my responsibility to guard it. Adults were strange with their punishments and even at seventeen, they still intimidated me. Right now, my mind was completely focused on doing and saying whatever I could to stay in Kelly's good graces; to keep Corrine in my dreams.

Unaware of my internal struggle, Doctor Kelly continued on with her explanation of what was happening between myself and Corrine. "What you are experiencing wid dis girl is somezing called shared dreaming—or dreamscaping," she said. "Here, let me show you."

A horseshoe magnet appeared in Kelly's palm. She held out her other hand and another magnet was revealed.

"Da brain naturally creates a magnetic field," she said. "But dis magnetic field is only so strong."

Kelly brought the magnets slowly together in front of her. Only once they got to be about an inch apart did the two actually hook together.

"See? Like magnets, human brains normally need to be very close to each odder in order to connect dese fields."

Like a magician, Kelly flipped her left hand and the magnet in that hand disappeared.

"Da talisman has enhanced your natural magnetic field—meaning you can easily travel to whatever place your mind is zinking about. Or, as in your case, any person your mind is zinking about."

Kelly lifted the remaining magnet so that the ends of the horseshoe pointed down the tunnel; as she did this the ground beneath us began to move.

"What the—?" I tried to look down at my feet, but my head was suddenly thrown back. The dusty earth beneath us jerked to life, racing forward like a giant conveyor belt. It picked up speed quickly, going faster and faster until the point where it felt as though we were being carried down the tunnel at the speed of light.

Out of the corner of my eye I could see Doctor Kelly still holding the magnet straight out in front of her. I tried to turn in her direction but the force of the wind made it nearly impossible. It was like trying to walk a straight line through a hurricane.

Turning my eyes forward again, up ahead what seemed to be an end to the tunnel appeared. Absolute terror gripped me as my brain registered what was happening. We were barreling toward it with such force that there was absolutely no way we were going to be able to stop in time.

An agonizing scream formed deep in my chest.

Shutting my eyes tightly, just as we were about to slam into it, I opened my mouth and the sound that came out was nothing short of–

"Ping!"

-surprising.

The magnet made the most delicate little noise, like a finger tapping on a wine glass, as it clicked softly against the filmy end of the tunnel.

Despite having the sensation that we were still moving, when I opened my eyes, I found our bodies were standing perfectly still.

I let out a high-pitched "I just learned I'm not going to die" kind of breath.

"Sorry," Kelly said with a smirk. "But you kind of deserved dat."

She turned back to where the magnet connected to the end of the tunnel and looked out.

On the other side of the translucent screen, Corrine was walking through the salvage yard.

As soon as I saw her, I ducked and hid behind Doctor Kelly. "Can she see us?" I whispered.

She stepped to the side and smiled. "No. She cannot see us. She cannot hear us. We are neidder here nor dere."

"Shared dreaming is not an easy zing to do on its own," Kelly added. "I don't know what your connection is wid dis girl, but our world is far harder to enter. Wid how new you are to all of dis, she should not be able to enter widdout da talisman."

Kelly explaining how difficult shared dreaming was certainly eased my fears over Terry being able to get into the dreams, but I still scanned the yard looking for him. All I could see was Corrine. My eyes widened.

"Have—have you been watching us?"

Kelly threw her head back and laughed a hearty laugh. "I'm not spying on you, if dat's what you're worried about. Members of da Lucid are able to connect if dey want to, but for da most part everyone here is enjoying deir own reality. Dis—" she said, pointing to Corrine, "— is yours."

I watched Corrine as she looked in and around the old cars out in the yard. She appeared to be calling out for me.

Suddenly curious, I turned to Doctor Kelly. "What's your reality?" I asked.

Kelly gave a somewhat pained smile. "It's da same concept as yours, really," she said, "but it's a little harder for some to understand."

I gave her a puzzled look.

Doctor Kelly reached down and grabbed one of my hands. She waved her free hand in front of us; through the filmy tunnel, a beach scene appeared. A man was throwing a Frisbee to a young boy and girl. They were all laughing, the waves crashing behind them. I recognized them right away from the picture that had been in Doctor Kelly's office.

"We all come here to enjoy, experience, and learn from da zings we are unable to in our real lives," she said.

"Isn't that your family?"

She nodded.

"Why can't you enjoy them in real life?"

Kelly turned to me. "Because dey're dead, Travis."

Chapter 14

The hair on my arms stood on end as we watched the man lift the little boy onto his shoulders. A deep cold crept into my bones as I watched the little girl, who happily bounded after them.

Doctor Kelly waved her hand in front of me, creating a warm lined jacket over my t-shirt. I wasn't about to tell her that she'd mistaken my goosebumps for being cold.

"It isn't really dem," Doctor Kelly said quietly. "Just my memories of dem." She turned to face me.

I noticed that she was now wearing a thick cream colored sweater.

"It gets cool out here in da evening, doesn't it?" A gust of cold air blew her hair all around her face.

I watched with a heavy sadness as she tried to tuck it back behind her ears.

"Most people don't like how chilly it gets at night, but dis was always our favorite time to be out here. We had da beach all to ourselves."

While the pristine memories of her once perfect family played out in front of us like a movie, I felt horrible as I thought about what I'd said in her office the week before. I'd said that I could tell she never really had to deal with anything before—something like that.

How wrong I'd been.

"What happened to them?" I asked sheepishly.

"A car accident—it's been almost seven years now."

"Is that how you got that scar?"

Kelly self-consciously touched the spot above her right eye and nodded with a faraway look. "Dat's how I became part of da Lucid. I had no interest in trying da talisman for myself until den. And who knows?" she added. "It might not have worked for me before den. My desire wouldn't have been strong enough."

She turned back to her family. "You see, I was already living in what, for me, was a perfect world." There was a hint of shame in her voice.

"I know a lot of people wouldn't agree wid dis. But if dey lost da people dey loved da most and were suddenly given da opportunity, if nodding else, to at least see deir faces again? I wonder how many of dem would say no."

I silently agreed.

"I don't come here to pretend dat dey are alive," she said quietly. "Dey are gone, and I am at peace wid dat. What I come here for is to remember dem when I feel alone."

"I'm sorry."

Kelly smiled kindly. "I know you are."

She looked out at her family once more and fondly blew them a kiss. As she waved goodbye, the picture was wiped away with her hand and replaced once again with my dream, where Corrine was still searching the salvage yard for me.

"Dere is a reason I asked if da two of you liked it here, Travis. When you have a lucid dream, you are exercising a certain part of your mind dat is seldom used. It becomes stronger and, in essence, you are permanently altering da chemistry of your brain every time you dream."

"What does that mean?"

"It means dat because of your connection wid da talisman, you are one of us now—one of da Lucid. You don't need da talisman anymore. You can come here anytime you want."

Kelly motioned to Corrine. "On da odder hand, she still has a choice."

"You mean she can be part of the Lucid, too?"

"Not in da sense dat she would have her own reality," Kelly answered. "Because she was brought here by you, she would become part of your reality."

"You mean every time I sleep—?"

Doctor Kelly finished my thought "—she would be here wid you."

"Forever?"

"As long as you boz are alive, yes, you would be tied togedder in your dreams."

My eyes bulged. As much as I wanted to spend the rest of my life with Corrine, I couldn't imagine her wanting to do the same with me.

"But—you said she has a choice?"

"Her tie to da talisman is not as strong as yours," Kelly explained. "If she stops meeting you here, she will go back to exactly how she was before—but if she continues? Den da choice will be made for her."

Incredulous, I asked, "So …what are you saying then? To keep her out of my dreams, I can't think about her? Is that it?"

Kelly chuckled. "We do expect you to be able to exercise some sort of self-control, yes."

"What if I can't?"

The levity in her voice left and she issued a stern warning. "It's not fair to play wid odder people's lives, Travis. Your decisions and actions do play a role in dis girl's future right now."

I started to panic. All I ever thought about was Corrine. I couldn't keep her from my thoughts for a minute, let alone the rest of my life. "I mean it, Doctor Kelly. What if I can't? What then?"

Doctor Kelly looked out at Corrine. A dark shadow crossed her face. "Dere is only one odder way...."

"What is that?"

"Da person who possesses da talisman not only has da power to bring odders in—dey can also cast dem out."

"Ah-ha!" I thought triumphantly. So there was a way to get rid of Terry if he found a way into the dreams!

"How do I do it?" I asked. "How do I get rid of someone I brought into the dreams?"

"By cracking da bloodstone."

She turned me around so that I faced her and placed her hands my shoulders. "Once da stone is cracked, da power of da stone is released. Dis is an act dat has great repercussions."

"What kind of repercussions?"

"For one, da talisman would be destroyed," She said. "But also da person who possesses da talisman would lose all ties to da dream world."

"So I couldn't get back in?"

"Not only would you not be allowed back in, but you would also lose all memories dat are connected to your time here."

Kelly turned my body around to face Corrine. "And so would she. All of da conversations dat you have had wid me, and all of da conversations dat you have ever had wid her about dis world, would be erased. It would be as if it never happened."

"Cracking da bloodstone is only to be used in da event dat something evil or unwanted gains entry into da Lucid." Kelly added after a beat. "A situation like dis certainly shouldn't warrant such drastic measures."

"This situation might not," I thought. But Doctor Kelly didn't know about Terry. If he found a way into the dreams the situation could become a lot worse. It wasn't fair! I couldn't win! Now I had to tell Corrine to stop meeting me in the dreams or risk her being trapped there with me forever? She'd never choose to stay with me! And Terry? The only way to get rid of him would mean breaking the talisman, assuming I could even get it back. And if I broke the talisman, all of our memories would be erased; it would be as if Corrine and I had never met. Why did every solution have to end with me being left alone?!

"How soon do I have to tell her?" I asked.

Kelly crossed her arms. "It's hard to say, but every time she comes here she is in greater danger of becoming trapped. If I was you, I would talk to her about it right now. I wouldn't wait."

At seventeen-years-old, I was stuck somewhere between having the mind of a child and the mind of a man. And right now, the childish part of my brain was winning out. I knew Kelly was right and I didn't want to hurt Corrine. I just wanted to keep her around a little longer. Could there really be much harm in that?

I watched Corrine spinning slowly around the salvage yard. Her hands were cupped around her mouth and I could faintly hear her calling my name through the screen.

I would tell her, I would. I promised myself. *–just not yet.*

"She very well may choose to stay here wid you," Kelly said, completely unaware of my intense internal struggle. "You are part of da

Lucid now and as you yourself said—who wouldn't like it here? You are boz welcome in dis world. But she needs to know how serious of a decision dat is."

Kelly nodded toward Corrine. "She's a beautiful girl," she said. "I can see why you're so taken wid her."

My face flushed and I looked down.

"Go to her," she said. "Talk to her about it. Time is nothing to play wid right now. Like I said, if you boz continue to meet here, da decision will be made for her."

As I looked back up from the ground the tunnel vanished— Doctor Kelly along with it. I was left standing only about twenty feet away from Corrine.

Chapter 15

She was one syllable into my name as she rotated a step in my direction. Corrine stopped yelling as soon as she saw me. "Where have you *been*? I've been calling your name for like ten minutes!"

Corrine looked around her with disdain, obviously disappointed in the choice. "Why a junk yard?"

"I didn't—" The words stopped as I realized what I was about to do.

"You didn't what?" She was looking at me with such trust; such honesty. Although she was wearing the same clothes she had been wearing earlier in the day something about how she looked now was absolutely radiant.

"I didn't—know where you wanted to go."

I felt a strong pang of guilt as I said this. It was wrong and I knew it, but it was thrilling to think that at this moment I had the opportunity to stay with her forever; even though it was only because she hadn't been given the choice yet.

"Well, there's nowhere to go from here but up." Corrine joked. She blushed and looked down at the ground, kicking at the dust with her feet.

The way she was acting gave me the feeling that my appearance was once again altered in the dream. And it suddenly made me angry. Why couldn't she look at me like that in the real world? I felt the fire from earlier in the day reignite in my belly as I thought about Terry and how he said I wouldn't know what to do with a girl like Corrine. It grew stronger still as I thought about Doctor Kelly and her absurd notion that Corrine might actually choose to stay here with someone like me. Why was I never good enough?

"What? Not good enough for you?" I asked roughly. "Name a place. Any place. I can take you anywhere you can think of."

Corrine looked up startled by the tone of my voice.

Seeing her reaction to me, knowing I knew things about the dreams that she didn't, and knowing that I actually had some sort of control over her life at this very moment—gave me a frightening sense of power.

To hell with it, I thought. I grabbed her by the hand and whipped her body away from me.

Using the same trick Doctor Kelly had used on the beach, as she twirled outward, I changed Corrine's plain jeans and t-shirt into a body hugging ball gown—the color of dried blood.

When she stopped she looked down at her dress in amazement. I looked at her too and the way the dress clung to her body made the fire inside of me rage out of control. My grip on her hand tightened. I squeezed it so hard that her fingers began turning white. This wasn't like me at all! I was totally out of control. It was almost as if I felt some strange need to punish her for not loving me back the same way I loved her.

"Travis! What's going on? Let go! You're hurting—"

Before she could finish her thought a huge fissure ripped across the ground between us. Corrine stumbled forward and let out a scream.

The terror on her face brought me crashing back. What was I doing?! I loved this woman! I didn't want to frighten her like this. It wasn't Corrine I was mad at. I was taking out all of my own guilt and shame on her, so that I wouldn't feel so disgusted with myself.

"Hold on, Corrine! It's going to be okay! Just don't let go of my hand!" I screamed. Eyes wide, she held on tight as marble tiles pushed up through the cracked earth beneath us—their gold inlay gleaming in the sunlight.

The engines of the cars roared to life. Corrine's head jerked around in every direction as they drove on top of each other, metal grinding on metal, stacking upward, until they morphed into the giant white walls of a spectacular ballroom. Like the floors, the walls were adorned with gold as well. Large mirrors appeared next to arched doorways. Mythical beasts and beautiful women were sculpted into their elaborate frames right before our eyes.

Way above our heads the ceiling rounded off into an enormous domed skylight —and through it hundreds of stars flicked on like Christmas lights.

Corrine looked upward in awe. She was frozen an arms-length away from me in the spot I had spun her out to; still holding my hand.

Loosening my grip, I reeled her back into me and pulled her to my chest. "Dance with me." I said it softly, my apology buried in the subtext of the words.

Corrine looked up at me with an unease I'd never seen from her before. "There's no music."

The word "music" hadn't even fully escaped her lips when the din of string instruments filled the room. It sounded as though an entire symphony was in there with us. Amusement replaced the wariness on her face and Corrine rolled her eyes at me.

"I can't dance, Travis."

With my arm around her waist, I held her hand firmly and whispered, "You can do anything here."

Corrine shivered and leaned her head back to look at me. My newfound confidence seemed to intimidate her.

"Close your eyes."

She studied my face first, trying to decide whether or not I was telling the truth, then dutifully closed her eyes.

"You can dance." I said again. Pulling her by the waist, I began leading her into the slow basic steps of the waltz.

It was like walking. We didn't even think about what we were doing—it just happened. And as the music picked up so did our steps.

Corrine opened her eyes and smiled an incredulous smile. Her body moved effortlessly across the floor with the grace and precision of a classically trained dancer.

She reached down and lifted up the corner of her gown. We danced in great sweeping circles around the ballroom and Corrine threw her head back and whooped the faster we went. There were mirrors everywhere and I couldn't help it—every time we moved by one I stared at my reflection. I loved seeing how my new face and body looked next to hers. I was the person I had always dreamed of being; the kind of person that deserved to be with someone like Corrine.

When the song came to an end, I dipped her all the way to the floor in a dramatic finish.

As I held her there, she looked up at me and something in her smiled changed. "Dance with *me* now," she said with a sly grin.

A sweet and slow melody that was not of my doing began to play in the air around us.

"And the student becomes the teacher," I chuckled.

I lifted her back up and tried to take her hand to assume the proper dance position, but she stopped me. Not taking her eyes off of mine, Corrine brought both of my hands down to her waist. She stepped closer, her face within inches of my own, and circled her arms gently around my neck. Her movements were so slow and deliberate and yet they made everything inside of me race.

We swayed back and forth to the music, but the energy in the room had changed every bit as much as our steps. Instead of us circling around the room, the room was now spinning around us. Corrine came closer still and my feet stopped moving.

"What are you—"

Corrine lifted her chin and grazed her lips over my mouth. She moved her head around in such a way that it felt like tiny feathers brushing over my skin. Every now and then, she'd let her mouth linger on my own for a moment and it would send sparks of electricity shooting down my legs.

Her breath was so close and hot on my face that it made it impossible to keep from touching her. I had to know where this could go. I had to know what she felt like. Leaning in, I tried to kiss her, but Corrine pulled back and smiled, teasing me.

I groaned, took my hands off her waist, and grabbed her face with both hands. Pulling her to me, I kissed her so hard that I thought I was going to hurt her.

Corrine not only met my force, but actually overpowered it. Before I could register my surprise, Corrine pushed me backward until we crashed into one of the great walls of the ballroom. As she pinned me down with her arms, I heard the wall crack. The fracture widened, splintering all the way up to the top of the ceiling, as we continued to kiss.

There was a brilliant flash of lightning overhead, but I really didn't care. Instead, I rolled Corrine around and positioned her so that her back was now against the wall.

As I leaned into her the music in the room began to slow. It played off key, like a music box that was winding down, but it didn't matter to me. Instead, I ran my hands up Corrine's naked back, feeling her soft, exposed skin above her gown.

Corrine arched her back and pushed away from the wall long enough to give me access to the thin zipper at the small of her back. As I reached for it, I saw plaster dust falling from my hair. The whole room was crumbling down around us, but we hadn't even noticed, Nor did I care.

I could die—right here, right now—and not give a damn about it.

Thunder shook the entire ballroom as I slid my hands down the back of her dress. My hands were about halfway down when Corrine started pushing me away. "Stop," she said.

There was another flash of lightning as I tried to kiss her again.

"Stop, Travis. Wait a second. Stop it."

But I didn't understand. Did she not want me like I wanted her? She was sure acting like she was enjoying herself. What was I doing wrong?

"I said, STOP IT!" Corrine screamed, then used both arms to shove me off of her.

"What?" I stepped back from her panting. "What's wrong? What did I do?"

"Why are you acting like this?"

I stared at her dumbly. "I was just doing what I thought you wanted me to do."

"What I want you to do, is to not act like everyone else!" Corrine's eyes filled with tears and she pulled her dress up, holding it to her chest with her hands. "I'm sorry," she said brokenly. "I'm so sorry."

Corrine turned her head aside and shut her eyes tightly. When she opened them again, a door appeared inside of one of the arched entryways. "I'm so sorry, but I can't do this," she said.

Corrine took off running towards the door. It slammed shut as she passed through, causing great rifts to spread up the walls, across the ceiling, and into the glass of the domed skylight.

I took off after her, dodging huge pieces of falling plaster as I did. The cracks in the glass of the skylight made horrible popping noises as they radiated outward. I knew the whole thing was likely to give way before I even had a chance to try and open the door, but I couldn't give up.

I had to know what I'd done to upset Corrine so badly.

Crossing my hands over my face, I closed my eyes and took a giant leap of faith. The glass shattered behind me like millions of diamonds falling from the sky, but amazingly, I passed through the solid door without a single scratch.

I landed in a crouched position on a dark outdoor terrace. Like the ballroom, the terrace was also made of marble. It was wide and circled the entire structure. It was raining steadily, yet despite the darkness and the rain, I somehow could still see Corrine standing next to a huge pillar at the top of a concrete staircase. As I got up off the ground and made my way over to her, I could see that the steps behind her led down to some kind of garden below.

"Stay away from me! Just leave me alone, Travis!" she cried. She was soaking wet, yet I knew if I made a blanket, she'd probably not take it from me.

Worse yet, she held on to the pillar at the top of the steps as if it were her last hope of salvation. Which I also didn't understand.

"Just tell me what I did! Please, Corrine, I thought—you don't have to be afraid of me."

"You were acting like an animal in there!" She yelled above the rain. "I thought you were sweet. I thought you were different. I thought-"

"I thought that's what you wanted me to do!" I yelled back. Then added childishly, "You're the one who started it!"

"I didn't mean for it to go that far!" Corrine let go of the wall; still keeping her distance. "I mean—this isn't right!" she screamed. "Don't you get that? I don't know what this is! Is this real? Is this a dream? I mean, if we do something here, is it real? Are we supposed to…?"

Corrine sank to the ground and covered her face with her hands, her breath catching in her sobs. "I don't know.. if …I can …do this… with you …out there. I mean…not that you aren't…I just …I just don't know if I can do this with you."

I suddenly realized this wasn't just about me losing control with her—it was about her fear of losing control with me. And it wasn't fair for her to shoulder all of the responsibility. She had to know I was just as guilty of using her looks against her. "Look at me, Corrine. Look at me!"

Corrine looked up at me, rain streaking down her face, her eyes full of shame. "I really like you," she sobbed. "I do. I feel so stupid. It's just like, I don't know. It just feels like it might get complicated in real life, ya know? It's so stupid! I don't know why I just can't—"

I turned my face up towards the sky and screamed over the sound of the rain. "I don't care!" Then I yelled at the sky itself. "Stop this!"

Miraculously, the torrential downpour shut off like a faucet.

Wide-eyed and terrified, Corrine looked at me as if she'd never seen me before.

I really didn't want her to be afraid, no matter how many strange powers I'd learned to use while she was away. That's why I lowered my voice before I pleaded with her, "Please, just listen to me."

I walked across the terrace to her, my legs feeling heavy and tired. As the last of the raindrops fell, I took a seat next to her at the top step of the staircase.

Folding my hands in my lap, I kept my eyes fixed on the stairs below. "I'm sorry I got carried away in there. If I'm not acting the right way, it's because I don't know how to act. I've—I've been in love with you since the first time I saw you," I said.

Corrine choked back a sob.

"Since the first time I *saw* you," I repeated. "Do you get that?"

I looked up at her. "Corrine, do you really think I would have felt that way if you looked like me?"

She shook her head, unable to answer.

I hated to make this admission, but it was the truth. Which was what Corrine deserved, no matter what she thought of me afterward.

"I've done the exact same thing to you that you've done to me."

"That's not what I was trying to say," she croaked.

"Yes, it is. The world's obsessed with what's on the outside, isn't it?" I rubbed my knee and chuckled humorlessly. "Can you imagine… can you even fathom how many dreams have been ruined, loves have been lost, opportunities missed? All based on something as silly as…"

"So we're both awful people. I get it," she whimpered.

"No," I said. "We're not. That's just part of who we are. Part of who we've been taught to be."

I grabbed her hands and turned by body toward her. "But we don't have to be like that here. Like you said, we can be who we really are in the dreams. We can change anything that bothers us."

"What are you saying, Travis?"

"I'm saying that I don't mind if we just have a relationship in the dreams."

She pulled her hands from mine. "And what? We ignore each other in real life? That's crazy!"

"Who says that has to be our real life? This can be our real life. I don't know about you, but this feels a hell of a lot more real to me than anything out there does."

Corrine became very quiet as she considered this. She looked down the steps at the moonlight hitting the grass below, at what was left of the ballroom behind us, and then at me. Wiping the tears from her eyes, she said earnestly, "We don't even know how long this is going to last."

This was my opening to tell her about what Doctor Kelly had said, but I didn't. We were breaking through something bigger than us. We were starting to see each other and like each other for who we really were. I wish I had had the guts to believe that this bond would have continued without the dreams, but I was also learning something very important about being young and in love—it could make you selfish. What had happened between us in the ballroom was like the most addictive drug I could have ever tried. It didn't matter how dangerous, dishonest, or wrong it was, I would do or say anything for the chance to feel that way again.

"We don't have to decide anything right now," I lied. "Let's just take this slow. See what happens."

Corrine grabbed my fingers and gave them a light squeeze. "We're still friends, right?" she asked.

"Still friends."

She smiled that sweet and honest smile. And the kindness in her eyes made me feel momentarily sick to my stomach.

Corrine bumped her shoulder against mine. "So… that rain trick you did was pretty cool. You wanna show me how you…" she stopped mid-sentence and turned to look back over her shoulder.

"What is that?"

"What?"

"Don't you hear it?" Corrine got up and started walking back toward the ballroom.

"Hear what?"

"Wait a second."

Corrine put her hand up and listened. "That's weird. I could have sworn I heard something."

"What?" I asked again.

"Whistling. Didn't you hear it? It sounded like somebody was whistling."

Chapter 16

It's amazing how quickly we fell into the pattern: moving through the days like they were dreams, waiting for our real lives to begin when the sun went down.

Every night that week, after she got off work, Corrine would sneak up to my apartment—her arms full of books.

We'd sit on the floor for hours scanning their pages, looking for places we wanted to go.

She'd begged to see the talisman on more than one occasion, but I lied and said that I had hidden it. I told her I didn't think it was safe for her to touch–that I didn't know what all it could do to her (which was probably the most honest thing I actually said.)

On Thursday afternoon, Corrine called me from the store and surprised me by asking if she could spend the night.

I tripped over my words into the receiver. "Wha—? Why?"

"I'm dragging at work," she said. "We've been staying up so late. I just thought if I stayed with you, then I'd be closer to the shop and—and I don't know? It would just be easier that way, that's all."

It was one thing, her coming over, but sleeping in my room? What did that mean?

We hadn't kissed or anything since the ballroom, but I knew we both had looked at each other often, just little glances, in the dreams—and we kept making excuses to touch each other. Did her wanting to spend the night mean she wanted to be more than friends?

"Travis? Are you there?"

"Yeah, I'm sorry," I said. "I'm here."

"Look, if you don't want me to...."

"No!" I exclaimed, then collecting myself. "It's not that. It's just, I don't think my parents would go for it, that's all."

Corrine laughed. "Oh, don't worry about that. They haven't seen me yet, right? I'm just gonna tell my parents that I'm spending the night at Marissa's."

"So it's cool?" she asked.

She had it worked out so well that I couldn't think of anything to do, other than to agree.

※※※

I made sure that my parents had dinner ready early, but couldn't bring myself to eat when I went down there.

"For having rushed me like you did, you sure weren't very hungry," my mom said as she cleared the table. "You hardly touched your food."

"I know. I'm sorry. I guess my eyes were bigger than my stomach."

She kissed me on the top of my head as she picked up my plate. "That's okay, honey."

"You've been pretty busy lately," Dad chimed in. "What have you been up to up in that room of yours?"

"His apartment," Mom corrected with a smile.

"Nothing much. Just working and stuff."

I couldn't stop fidgeting with my napkin at the table. Afraid it was going to betray my nervousness; I got up and started helping my mom with the dishes.

"That's so nice of you, Travis! Thank you."

"You know you're really growing up," Dad said from the table. "I mean it. I see a big change in you these days."

"Ah, I don't know about that, Dad." I wiped the water off the counter with a dish rag, then hurried over to the front door to put my shoes on.

"Where are you going?" My Mom asked.

"I have to get my comforter," I said. "I put it in the dryer before dinner."

My Mom put her hand to her chest. "That's it," she said. "Who are you, and what have you done with my son?"

I rolled my eyes, "I'm still your son."

If only she knew the reason I was washing it was because I had a girl coming over, and that I needed to get all the blood stains out of it from my fight with Terry. I wondered how proud she'd be then.

Just to be extra safe, as I left, I stuck my head back in the door and said, "Hey, I'm watching this really cool science fiction marathon tonight, so I kinda don't wanna be bugged, okay?"

"Oh, can we *please* watch it with you?" Dad joked.

"Ha. Ha. Dad."

Then as I shut the door, I called out, "See ya tomorrow!"

Chapter 17

Corrine arrived just after seven as she always did. I quickly jumped up to lock the door behind her. "Did anyone see you?" I asked.

"Nope. Coast is clear." She held up a paper sack from the store. "Want a bagel?"

I ripped the bag out of her hands. "Yeah, I'm starving!"

Corrine tried to grab it back, but I held it up over my head.

"Hey, Come on!" She laughed. "I want one, too!"

We started researching places we wanted to go that night. About an hour into our research, Corrine looked up from her book and said, "Terry's acting kinda weird."

I took my fingers off the keyboard to my computer, where I had ironically been searching for images of "dream vacations." "What do you mean?"

Corrine's mouth was full of bread as she answered, "I don't know. I think he knows I'm coming over here or something."

The idea of Terry knowing she was here made me very nervous. I swiveled in my chair to face her. "Why would you think that?"

Corrine put her hand up and took a moment to swallow. She took a sip of soda and then answered, "He keeps coming over to the store and he just kind of … stares at me." Corrine shrugged her shoulders. "I don't know how else to explain it."

"Hmph." I considered this, but her theory wasn't exactly based on hard evidence. And I had done such a good job of pushing Terry from my mind that there seemed no reason to stop now. "It's probably nothing."

Corrine stared at me a minute. "Yeah, you're probably right."

Before she looked back down at her book, I thought I saw a brief glimmer of something in her eyes. Was it distrust? Could she tell I was keeping something from her? It made my jaw tense and a lump rise in my throat. I wanted her to trust me. She needed to know the truth. Since Terry hadn't posed any kind of real threat to us yet, I didn't necessarily feel the need to tell her about him, but she needed to know what would happen to her if she kept meeting me in the dreams. As I looked at her, part of me wondered if it was too late already.

"Oh my gosh!" she exclaimed.

"What?" Her outburst startled me and I jumped up from my chair.

"This is where I want to go tonight!"

I walked up behind her and looked over her shoulder. When I saw what she was looking at, I breathed a sigh of relief. It was a picture of the earth from space.

"You want to go to space?" I asked, amused.

"Sure, why not?" Corrine shrugged like she was suggesting we go to the bank.

Leaning over her shoulder I touched the page with my finger and said, "We can make it better than that."

She smiled up at me, her eyes dancing with anticipation.

"I'm going to tell her," I thought. "I'm going to tell her the truth tonight; surrounded by the most beautiful surroundings my mind can possibly create." I thought maybe, just maybe if I made it beautiful enough, Corrine wouldn't be able to say no; that she would agree to stay in the dreams with me forever.

ఌఞ

I let Corrine have the sofa that night. But I wasn't that far away, as I had curled up with a blanket on the floor next to her. When we entered the lucid state, we were still in the same positions, but the floor and futon beneath us had been swapped out for a cold and uncomfortable slab of stone.

The sound of water rushing behind us is what awoke us to the dream. We were right in the center of a great temple made entirely of stone. Four huge pillars held up its massive rectangular roof and there must have been at least a hundred steps leading up to it from the ground below.

Corrine was the first to get to her feet. She took her time doing so, almost as if she were afraid she'd miss something if she didn't. I quickly followed.

The temple was on a floating island in space, like a tiny undiscovered planet. Its rocky terrain was covered with a thick layer of green moss and large beads of moisture glimmered across its surface like crystals. Behind the temple coursed a wide and powerful waterfall. Stars shone brilliantly all around us.

Right in front of us—from inside the temple—we had the most amazing view of the earth, a gigantic, glowing blue sphere that took up our entire field of vision.

"This is too cool," breathed Corrine.

We had come to find that the sky was always one of the most beautiful things to look at in the dreams. Here, the upper atmosphere had color and dimension that was nearly impossible to put into words. It was like the Northern Lights on steroids.

"I don't even think astronauts ever had this good a view." I said.

"Wait." Corrine turned to me, her profile illuminated by the glow of the earth. "Why aren't we weightless?"

I stretched out a hand toward her. "We can be if you want."

She smiled and lifted her arm so that our fingertips touched.

We were two silhouettes standing in front of the world.

"Ready?" I asked.

Corrine nodded and bit her lower lip. We closed our eyes, and together, our bodies lifted gently, effortlessly off the ground.

As we neared the top of the temple, we stopped. Corrine raised her eyebrows, clenched her teeth and let go of my hand with a nervous look of excitement.

Suspended in the air next to her, I watched with amusement as she worked up the courage to wiggle her fingers and toes.

"Oh my God!" she squealed. "Look! I'm doing it!"

"You think that's cool? Watch this!" I threw myself back and did a reverse somersault in the air. It was the most incredible feeling, like swimming or flying.

Trying to copy me, Corrine tipped herself forward and let out a high-pitched shriek as she tumbled around.

I zoomed towards her, but Corrine pushed me back out, laughing.

Becoming more confident we circled each other in the air, giggling like children.

"Hey! Have you ever been on roller skates?" Corrine asked. "You know, how you hold hands and spin around in a circle with someone?"

"Like this?" I'd never been on skates, but I knew what she was talking about. I'd seen plenty of other kids do it.

"Yeah!" She grabbed my hands and we kicked our legs in the air to get ourselves moving.

Once we'd built up some momentum, Corrine told me to pull her hands in. "That's how you go faster!"

She pulled back on my hands at the same time with the same force and we whirled around like a top. The faster we went, the closer we got. With our foreheads touching, Corrine threw her arms around my neck and held on tight.

I thought she was afraid she was going to fly away if she let go, but as the rotation slowed, she still held fast.

"I have a surprise for you," I said when we stopped.

"What could be better than this?!"

"This is totally better. I promise."

"Uh oh!" Corrine squealed with delight. "What is it?"

"Close 'em."

She closed her eyes.

I floated back so that just our fingertips were touching.

"What are you doing?" Corrine hung suspended in the air; she was biting her bottom lip and grinning from ear to ear.

When I was ready, I floated closer and laced her fingers in mine. "Okay, you can open them now."

Corrine's eyes flew open and she looked around. "What?" she asked. "What is it? What did you do?"

"Hold on a second," I said. "It's coming."

She jumped as a beam of light zipped behind my head. There was another, and another—until hundreds of balls of warm, yellowish light began to fall down all around us.

"What are they?" she breathed. "Are they shooting stars?"

"It's the moonlight," I said. "It's raining moonlight."

Corrine looked around us absolutely spell-bound. "Flowers are so over-rated."

I couldn't take my eyes off of her; laughing, the moonlight streaking behind her. She seemed to glow. And for the first time it wasn't her physical beauty I was seeing, I was seeing her spirit. She was fearless; full of joy, life, and— magic. That was it! That was what really drew me to Corrine. There was something magical about who she was that had nothing to do with the dreams at all.

"This is so beautiful," Corrine gasped.

"I've never seen anything more beautiful in my entire life," I said directly to her.

Corrine focused in on me. It felt as though she was looking all the way inside of me.

I didn't know if it was because we were floating or what, but I felt a lightness take over, like everything that had ever bothered me just lifted right out.

"Kiss me, Travis." She pulled herself into me and searched my eyes. "I want you to kiss me."

I had been hoping, praying, and wishing every second of every day that this would happen again. But as I brought my mouth softly to hers, I found that this kiss was entirely different than what we had shared in the ballroom. It was sweet, and kind, and an expression of everything good and wonderful there was about life.

She kept her eyes closed and pressed her lips together as I pulled back.

"I wish we could just freeze time right now," she whispered. "That we could just stay like this forever."

Looking at her like this and feeling what I felt in this moment, I hated myself. How could I have done anything so vile and so wrong to such a beautiful creature? Here she was kissing me, but I had been risking her entire future for my own personal gain. She deserved to know the truth. It was time to tell her about what Doctor Kelly had said to me.

I drew her hands into my chest.

"Corrine? Open your eyes, Corrine. I have something I have to tell you."

"Mmm," She hummed. "You can tell me anything."

"No. It's really important."

Corrine opened her eyes halfway; her lids heavy.

Summoning all of my courage, I took a deep breath. "What if we could?"

"What if we could what?"

"What if we could stay like this forever?" I asked.

"Wouldn't that be wonderful?" Her tone was dreamy and unbelieving.

"No. I'm serious. Look, Corrine-"

She lifted my arm. Giggling, she spun herself underneath like we were dancing. After she finished her spin, I gripped both her hands firmly in front of me. Corrine tipped her head back and laughed.

"Corrine, listen to me."

She straightened up and gave me a mock serious look. "Okay, Okay. I'm listening." She pursed her lips together, but a few more giggles escaped as she waited for me to speak.

How was I going to say this? She wasn't taking me seriously at all. Best to be blunt, I thought. I just needed to come out and say it.

"Corrine," I started again. "Corrine, if you don't stop coming here with me-if you don't stop having these dreams with me—you're going to …"

Before I could finish, something buzzed between us. It hit my shoulder. The force of it knocked the two of us apart.

"What the heck was that?" Corrine shrieked.

It flew between us again. This time, I saw it. A shadow, small and compact; the size of a soccer ball. We followed it with our eyes as the shadow disappeared behind one of the columns below.

"What was that?" she asked again. "Was it a bird?"

"It sure didn't feel like a bird," I said. "Come on." I pulled Corrine down in the direction it had gone.

We landed softly on the ground and padded around the floor of the temple.

"There's that sound again," she said.

My skin began to crawl as I heard the whistling noise that Corrine had first described outside the ballroom. The sinister discordance of that tune could only belong to one person.

"It sounds almost like—" Corrine stopped.

"Corrine, I have to tell you something!"

"Shhh," she whispered. She put her arm out to block me from moving. "Listen. Do you hear that?"

We both turned to face the waterfall at the same time.

"It sounds louder, doesn't it?"

Just as Corrine said this, the water picked up with great intensity. We stepped back, the spray hitting us. It was barreling down with five times the force it had before. The rush of the water captivated us both.

The temple began to shake under our feet. There was a terrible scraping sound as the pressure from the water moved the great stone roof above. It looked like it was going to fall directly on top of us.

I grabbed Corrine's hand. "Run!"

We quickly made a break for the stairs, but water was already pooling around them below, quickly rising to meet us.

"What's going on?!" Corrine screamed. "Make it stop!"

"We need to calm down," I said. I squeezed her hand and closed my eyes as the water thundered down around us.

"Stop!" I yelled.

Nothing.

I kept my eyes shut tight.

"Corrine, help me! Close your eyes! Help me change it!"

She was leaning into me so hard that it was making it impossible to concentrate. "Travis, Look!"

Corrine yanked my arm down in terror. The water was still rising, but when I opened my eyes I saw what was truly alarming Corrine.

A figure had appeared about fifty feet in front of us. It was a massive black shadow in the shape of a person, but it was twice the size of both of us. It walked slowly and purposely on top of the water, its arms outstretched like a tight-rope walker.

"What is that?"

"Corrine, close your eyes now!" I barked.

"No!" she screamed. She was completely beside herself. "I want to wake up! I want to wake up right now!"

Corrine put her hands over her ears, closed her eyes, and screamed as loud as she could. It was a deafening cry that pierced all the way through the air into my mind.

And just like that, we were ripped out.

Corrine shot up from the futon in my apartment, panting.

Still buzzing from the adrenaline in the dream, I leapt up from the floor to be by her side.

"Are you okay?"

She nodded vigorously, trying to catch her breath.

"What happened?"

I sat next to her and rubbed her back with my hand.

"I don't know." I said, although I did.

Terry had found his way into the dreams.

I knew that all of the things I had been avoiding were about to culminate into one impossibly real nightmare from which there would be no escape.

"Maybe it was just a bad dream?" I said. Which was true, wasn't it? Besides, it was the only way I could think to describe to her what had happened until I could come up with a plan.

"A bad dream?"

"Yeah," I said. "I guess even these kinds of dreams don't always go the way that you want."

Chapter 18

We never went back to sleep that night. We were afraid we'd pick up where we left off.

In the morning, Corrine decided to take a quick shower across the hall before she left for work. While she was in there, I paced the room. I still needed to tell her everything and there wasn't much time. I also knew I was going to need her help with Terry. I'd have to tell her about him first. Surely, she wouldn't want to help me with him after she found out about what I had done to her.

While I was formulating my plan, a key began to turn in the lock of my door.

"Honey?"

I came shooting across the room to try and stop them, but my parents pushed past me, their arms full of plates and Tupperware containers.

"Mom! Dad! What are you doing here?"

"Well what kind of greeting is that?" Mom asked. "Why is the water on? We thought you were in the shower."

I desperately tried to push them back out the door, but they didn't budge.

"I was just about to get in!" I said. "Lemme just jump in real quick and then I'll come down."

"We can wait." Dad said, pulling out a chair. He opened one of the containers and popped a piece of bacon in his mouth. "Your mom went to a lot of trouble to make you this breakfast, son. You should act a little more appreciative."

"You've been so great, honey!" My mom held up a large plate stacked with pancakes. "I made your favorite," she chirped. "Banana!"

"You shouldn't have."

"Oh, I wanted it to be a surprise," she said, faking humility. "Now, your Dad said I should call you first, but like I told him, who doesn't like a good sur–"

The water shut off in the bathroom and their heads whipped toward the hallway in startled unison.

"—prise. What was that, honey? Did the water just shut off?"

I started picking up the dishes, desperately trying to hand them back to my parents.

"I'm so sorry, guys. Now's really not a good time." Before I could come up with any kind of explanation, Corrine called out from the bathroom.

"Travis? Were you just talking to me?"

My parent's mouths dropped open.

"Is someone? Is that—?" My mother stumbled a few times before she actually got it out, "Travis? Do you have a girl over here?"

My father shot up from the table. "Come on, Catherine, maybe we should give the kid some privacy."

"Are you serious?" she bellowed. "Sit down. We're not going anywhere. This is completely unacceptable. For God's sake, he's a teenager!"

My Dad was about to say something back when the bathroom door opened. It was directly across the hall and with my door wide open there was nowhere she could run without being seen.

All three of us froze, waiting to see what would happen next.

Corrine stepped out slowly. Her hair was wet and thrown back in a ponytail. She had on the same jeans and shirt she had come over in the night before. There were wet spots on them like she had just thrown them on without even having a chance to dry off first.

I held my breath waiting to see what she would do.

Not missing a beat she cheerfully called out, "Oh, hi!"

My dad's jaw dropped. My mother stammered a quick hello back.

"I'm sorry." Corrine walked over to them and extended a hand.

"I'm Corrine. You must be Travis' parents. How nice to meet you."

My dad pumped her arm up and down with great enthusiasm.

"Sorry, I know this looks really bad," Corrine said. "Travis was helping me with a project for this summer program I'm taking. We were up really late and my parent's hot water is off so he was really nice and suggested I stay here. If I had known it was going to be a problem I never would have said yes."

She flashed her million dollar smile, rendering my father completely defenseless.

"No, no. No problem at all," he gushed. "Don't worry about it. We're glad to have you."

I envied Corrine's ability to lie on the spot like that.

"I'm actually on my way to work," she said. "I'm so sorry, I wish I could stay and chat some more."

My parents watched in stunned silence as she grabbed her signature cardigan off the floor. At least now Corrine could see where I had gotten my terrific communication skills from.

"So, it was nice meeting you," Corrine said, nodding to my parents.

"Yeah, you too!" my father blurted.

My mother elbowed him lightly in the side.

Corrine paused when she got to the door. "Um, so thanks for all your help, Trav."

I just smiled awkwardly at her and looked back and forth between my parents.

Corrine lightly chuckled to herself as she closed the door, leaving me to clean up the mess.

My mom's eyes narrowed as she walked out.

There was a long uncomfortable stretch of silence.

My father fell back in the chair and popped another piece of bacon in his mouth. "Well, I like her!"

"You would." My mom shot back. She put the lid back on the bacon and pushed it away from him.

"Travis, this apartment is for practice," she said. "You don't pay the bills here. You're still under our roof. As long as we pay the bills and you're still in school you have to abide by our rules."

She started looking around the apartment as if to make sure we were really alone.

"What were you thinking?" she said. "Why would you ever think we'd be okay with a girl spending the night here?"

"Oh, come on honey. It was an honest mistake," my dad said. "You heard the girl. Travis was just trying to be nice."

While my mom marched back and forth across the apartment, my dad got hold of the bacon again. He had a ridiculous smile plastered on his face. I could swear if his chest puffed out any further the buttons would come flying right off his shirt.

"And, that girl is a friend of yours?" my Mom asked.

"Yes, Mom."

"And she needed to use your shower?" She held out the word shower to emphasize how confused she was by the idea.

I just stood by my father; my eyes cast downward.

My mother moved opposite us and put her arms down on the table.

"If she was here for help with school, then where were her books? I didn't see her take a book bag with her. Travis, you're not giving this girl anything are you?"

My head snapped up. "What is that supposed to mean?"

My mother sighed; looking very annoyed with me.

"Well, she needed to use your shower so she obviously doesn't have any money."

"You can't be serious," I said.

My mom crossed her arms and shrugged her shoulders as if to say she didn't know.

Waking from his delirium my father started to get up from his chair. "Now Catherine, hold on a second here."

"Dad, stay out of this," I snapped.

My mother jumped at the tone of my voice.

"You think I'm paying her to be my friend?" I demanded. "Is that what you're saying?"

She uncrossed her arms and backed away as I moved toward her.

"What? You can't believe a girl would be interested in me?"

My mother shook her head.

"No, that's not what I meant," she said. "Of course I think a girl could be interested in you. It's just not a girl like–that."

"A girl like what?"

There was a long pregnant pause.

"Oh," I said. "I get it."

Staring her down, I said the words she could not bring herself to say. "Why would a girl who looks like that be interested in someone who looks like me?"

My mother froze. I could tell she hadn't even known that she'd felt that way until it was actually said out loud. My father walked up behind her and put an arm around her waist.

"No, that's not what I meant," she said.

"Then what exactly did you mean?" I asked dangerously.

My mom tried to move toward me, but my dad pulled her back.

"I'm just trying to protect you, Travis! Can't you see that?" she begged. "I'm your mother. I'm supposed to protect you. All I'm saying is I don't want to see you get taken advantage of—"

"Just stop it!" my father roared. "Both of you!"

Ashamed and defeated, I bowed my head. "I'm sorry, Mom. I really am," I said. "I shouldn't have had her over here. It not going to happen again, anyway."

"I think what we all need right now is to just calm down," Dad said, trying to be the voice of reason. "There's no reason to be sorry, Travis." He pulled my mother over to the door. "I think we should just all take a little break and cool down until we can talk about this in a more civilized manner."

I picked up the food they brought and handed the containers back to my father. "I'm not really hungry." I said.

He nodded and tucked what he could under his arm.

My mother looked stunned. Like she was replaying what had just happened over and over again in her head. I was the one who had clearly been in the wrong; having a girl secretly spending the night. How had the situation been turned around on her?

It made me hurt for her as much as I did for myself. "I'll come down in a little while." I said.

"No rush. Just come on down when you're ready." Dad gave a stern nod, then closed the door behind them.

I used my hands to brace myself on the table and hung my head.

Chapter 19

My parents hadn't even been gone for ten minutes when Corrine came crashing back through my apartment door.

She slammed it shut behind her, frantically working the lock.

"Why aren't you at work?" I asked, confused, still in a blur from what had happened.

Corrine ignored me and ran to the futon. Grabbing it by the base, she tried to drag it towards the door.

"Help me!" she cried. "He might be following me!"

"Who? Who's following you?" I got no answer.

"Corrine. Wait. Stop. Who's following you?" I asked again.

I ran over and tried to pry her hands back from the bed, but she fought me. As she leaped to get around to the other side of the futon, Corrine tripped and fell to the floor. She stayed there.

"He knows about us." Corrine covered her face with her hands and began to weep softly.

"What do you mean? Who knows about us?" I knelt down beside her and put a hand on her shoulder.

"Terry." Corrine shook her head from side to side. "He knows about us. He knows about the talisman. He saw us. He said he saw us dancing."

He saw us dancing? It's not like I hadn't known he was there, but I had no idea he'd been there so long! The idea of him seeing what had happened in the ballroom made my stomach turn.

I suddenly found it very hard to breathe. Scooting myself up onto the bed, I put my hands on my hips and bowed my head. It felt like the temperature of the room had been turned up twenty degrees.

"This isn't how I wanted you to find out."

"What?" Corrine's head snapped up in complete surprise. "What are you saying?"

"Terry has the talisman, Corrine. He stole it."

"You mean you knew about this?"

The admission opened a floodgate of emotions. "Oh, Corrine, I'm so sorry." I moaned. "I've done some really horrible things. I wanted to tell you, I did. I was going to tell you in the dream last night, but then he showed up and—"

"Wait? That was him?" she asked. "In the nightmare? That was Terry?"

"Yes," I said. "It was him in the dream last night."

"Why would you keep something like that from me?" Corrine looked around the room, her face filled with confusion and disgust. "How long has he had it? I mean, how much has he seen? Has he seen everything we've done?"

She brought her hands to her stomach as if she felt sick. "Oh my God. Some of those things were really private moments, Travis! You mean you knew he was watching us and you didn't tell me?! Why would you do that?"

Corrine slapped my leg hard with her hand. "Why would you do something like that?"

She tried to hit me again and I grabbed her by the wrist. "I didn't know he was there until last night!"

"But you said you knew he had the talisman?!"

"Yes, I did! But I didn't know he was in the dreams!" I let out a frustrated groan. "That's only part of this whole mess."

I decided to come clean. "Look, Corrine, I'm going to tell you everything, I promise. Right now though, what I need from you is to tell me exactly what Terry said to you."

৩○৩

Apparently, while I had been fighting with my mom and dad, Corrine had come face to face with some judgment of her own.

She said that maybe she would have seen it coming had she not been so amused by the way she had left me with my parents. As she walked from my apartment to the coffee shop, Corrine couldn't stop laughing–recalling how freaked out she'd been in the shower when she heard them come up, and how I'd looked at her like a deer caught in headlights when she walked out the door.

As she passed the alley, she remembered how nervous we'd both been when I first asked her to meet me there. She thought it seemed odd–just how recent that had been.

Just then, as she was lost in thought, she felt a hand on her arm. Corrine shrieked as she was pulled into the alleyway.

She tried to scream, but Terry clamped his hand firmly over her mouth and slammed her up against the brick wall. He pushed his full weight against her and whispered in her ear. "I know what you're doing."

He pulled back.

Corrine was terrified; her heart was pounding a mile a minute.

Terry licked his lips and pushed harder against her. "You're disgusting." With one hand still over her mouth he used his free hand to rip at her clothes. Terry dug into her pockets and then tore her shirt out of her jeans, moving his hands under her waistband.

"Where is it?" he hissed.

Corrine shook her head frantically to indicate she didn't know what he was talking about.

"The talisman, Corrine. I know there's another one."

She ripped his hand off her mouth, but he pressed his forearm against her throat. "I want the talisman." he said again. "If I have the only one, then why are you both still in the dreams? Where is it?"

She strained against the pressure to answer. "I don't have it."

Terry stared at her hard. "And all this time you acted like you were too good for my brother." With his arm still across her neck, Terry pulled his body back from Corrine. "Now I know you're just a freak, too."

He spit over his shoulder. "I saw you dancing with him. I saw what you were doing. You make me sick."

Realizing her lower body was now free, Corrine took advantage of the position and delivered a swift, hard blow to his groin.

As Terry doubled over in pain, Corrine took off like a shot out of the alley.

ಏಲ

She rocked back on her heels and her eyes took on a strange vacant quality as she replayed the scene. "I was so scared." Corrine said. "I know he's not the best person in the world—but that he could do something like that to me—that he could attack me like that? He really scared me. For a second I thought...."

As much as I wanted to comfort Corrine, her story only confirmed the seriousness of what was going on. If Terry had been in the dreams for this long and had the talisman, was he now part of the Lucid, too?

"Corrine, I'm so sorry I dragged you into all of this," I said. My voice took on a kind of confidence and control that I had never experienced outside of the dreams. "I know you don't understand any of this, but it's very important for both of us that we get the talisman back— that we get it back as soon as humanly possible. It might be too late already...."

"Too late for what? Travis, what's going on here? If he has the talisman? Why are we still in the dreams?"

"There's something else I've been keeping from you," I said. "Something I was going to tell you last night. Something I will tell you, I swear, but first we have to get that talisman back. Do you understand?"

Corrine raised one eyebrow suspiciously, "Why don't you tell me now?"

"Because you might not like me much after I do. And right now, I need your help. I can't do this on my own."

"I don't know if I like you that much now."

"I mean it, Corrine. Even if we can't get the talisman back, I'm going–I'm going to tell you everything."

"When?"

"Tonight. I'll tell you everything you need to know tonight," I said. "I have to start fixing everything I've messed up. And it starts with getting the talisman back."

"Tonight?"

"Tonight."

I put my hand out in front of her. "Will you help me?"

"Why should I?" she asked. "Give me one good reason."

"'Cause even if you don't want to help me, I know you'd still like to pay Terry back for what he did to you."

Corrine's eyes narrowed. She bounced her leg nervously up and down a couple of times as she considered this.

"Okay." She agreed.

Corrine thrust her hand forward. Gripping mine maybe a little too tightly, she asked, "So what, exactly, do you need me to do?"

Chapter 20

There were only two obvious places to look—the bar, and Terry's house. He and John shared a place together. Corrine knew where it was, so she drew me a map of how to get there. It wasn't far, just about a mile off Main Street.

Knowing it would be a death trap for me, Corrine agreed to cover the bar on her own.

She called John from my apartment first to see if Terry was there. When John said that he had gone on a supply run, Corrine saw her opening. Taking advantage of Terry's absence, and of John's feelings for her, Corri asked if she could come by right away and talk to him privately. She said she was worried about Terry. John, as expected, jumped at the bait.

Corrine kissed me on the cheek, "for good luck," she said, and hurried off to the bar.

༄༅

Terry and John rented a house on a quiet block in a residential neighborhood. It was a small, white, single family home in desperate need of a good power washing. The yard seemed just as neglected. There were more weeds than grass which grew up in huge clumps through the cracks in the concrete driveway.

As I approached the front door, I noticed there were no cars parked outside. Terry didn't have a garage either, but it still didn't ease my nerves. Giving the door a quick knock, I jumped back, ready to run in case he answered.

When he didn't, I gently reached down and tried the door. It was locked.

Beads of sweat formed on my brow. I wiped at them with my shirt as I leaned back and checked out the windows on the front of the house. Fearing I would be seen if I tried to get in that way, I decided to walk around to the back of the house.

In the backyard, I found a small, weathered porch that led up to a door at the back of the house. Scanning the neighboring yards, I made sure no one was looking, and then climbed cautiously up the steps. Again, I knocked.

Once again, there was no answer. But when I tried the door this time, my heart immediately began to race—it swung right open.

Stepping halfway inside I called out, "Hello?"

It was silent.

I hesitated a moment, then stepped all the way in. The door made a gentle clicking sound as I closed it behind me.

I was standing in what I could only assume was their dining area. There was a round wooden table littered with paper, beer cans, and cigarettes. To my right was the kitchen. Dirty dishes were piled up all over the counters. The floor was filthy; the linoleum curling up in the corners of the room.

As fast as I could, I opened up all of the drawers and cupboards in the kitchen. Coming up with nothing, I moved further into the house. The living room consisted of an archaic brown sofa and a television. Clothes were everywhere and there was a stale odor about the room. I picked shirts and pants up off the floor and shook them to see if the talisman had been stuffed into any of the pockets.

Their house may have been messy, but there really wasn't much to it, so it was fairly easy to search. I flipped on the hallway light and saw there were only two places I had left to look—the bathroom, and Terry's bedroom. John's bedroom was at the end of the hall; I saw no point to looking there.

I chose the bathroom first and felt a stir of hope when I opened the medicine cabinet and saw three small boxes. But my heart sank as I opened each one and found only two pairs of cufflinks—and a class ring.

Terry's room came as an equal disappointment. I checked his closet, nightstand, and dresser drawers, but still came up with nothing. Something, however, did catch my eye on a shelving unit next to Terry's bed.

He had a picture of Corrine.

I picked it up and stared at the photo. It appeared to have been cut in half. Corrine was staring directly into the lens, laughing. There was an arm around her shoulder, but the person whom that arm belonged to was missing.

I ran my finger lightly over her image. As I admired her beauty, a sound came from the other side of the house.

My body froze. I held my breath and listened carefully, then my stomach dropped and blood immediately shot up into my face as I realized the noise was the front door being opened. There was a heavy fall of footsteps in the living room, followed by the jingle of keys being tossed onto a hard surface.

My body jerked back and forth in panic. There was nowhere to run. The direction of the footsteps changed and my heart nearly stopped. They were now moving into the hallway towards me: it had to be Terry.

I dived under the bed and swung my legs under just as he reached the door. On my stomach, my palms pressed to the floor, I watched in terror as he stood in the entrance to the room. All I could see were his boots. He stood there for a few seconds and then slowly began walking in the direction of where I hid. Closing my eyes tightly, I balled my hands into fists, bracing myself.

Terry sat down on the bed and began taking off his shoes. The weight of his body pressed the mattress down so far that it actually touched my back. And my heart was beating so hard in my chest that I didn't know how it was that he couldn't hear it.

When his shoes were off, Terry stood up. I watched, paralyzed, as he moved across the hall into the bathroom.

I heard the shower turn on. From my position on the floor, I could only see his legs. Relief washed over me as I saw his pants fall around his ankles. When he gets in the shower, I'll have a chance to escape, I thought.

But that's when I saw it—in the jeans he had discarded on the floor. Sticking out of his left front pocket was the unmistakable round metal edge of the talisman.

Terry's feet stepped up and out of my line of sight. I heard the shower curtain close.

I knew I had to move fast. Summoning all of the courage I had, I moved out from under the bed. I was shaking so hard that my arms wobbled beneath me as I crawled toward the bathroom.

Keeping my eyes glued on the shower, I stopped at the doorway and stretched my arm forward. The jeans were close enough that I could reach them without actually going in.

But just as my fingers made contact with the talisman the shower curtain ripped back. Terry's arm reached out as he fumbled for a bottle of shampoo on the shelf above the toilet. He cursed as he knocked over a can of shaving cream.

The can landed right next to my hand. I flattened my body as close as I could to the floor.

Terry pulled the shampoo back into the shower, but left the curtain partially open. I could now see the back of his head under the running water. All he would have to do is turn his head to the side, and he would see me.

My fingers were still on top of the talisman. I closed my eyes and clenched my teeth as I tightened my grip, cringing at every rustle of movement as I carefully pulled it out of Terry's pants. On hands and knees, with the talisman held tightly in my fist, I carefully backed out of the bathroom.

Just to make sure he couldn't immediately follow me, I grabbed Terry's keys before quietly slipping out the back door and then down the steps.

Chapter 21

Corrine and I arrived back at my place at the same time. I waved the talisman in the air as I ran towards her on the street. "I got it!" I cried, holding the stone up over my head like a victory torch.

Her car was parked right in front of the building. Corrine threw herself down in the front seat as soon as she saw me and rolled down the window. "Come on!" she yelled. "Hurry up! Get in!"

As I ran around the side of the car she leaned over and opened the door for me. I barely had a chance to close it before she squealed out of the spot.

"Don't worry he can't follow us." I said, pulling Terry's keys out of my pocket and rattling them in the air.

"I know. But he knows you took them."

"He does?"

"Yeah. He called John a few minutes ago. I was there."

Corrine looked over at me smiling. "John and I just finished up quite the exciting little conversation."

ೞಚ

John was already standing outside of the bar eagerly awaiting her arrival when she had jogged up.

"Where did you come from?" he asked, looking up the street.

"Oh, I just had to get some stuff done," Corrine said, shrugging it off. "Mind if we go inside to talk? Maybe the office?" It was the most private room in the bar and the first place Corrine could think to look.

"Yeah, sure." John looked pleasantly surprised. "Come on in." He stepped aside to let her in and then led her past the bar to the room in the back they used as an office. Once inside, he closed the door behind them.

Corrine scanned the room. There were two desks positioned against opposite walls. One had newspaper clippings from John's football days and pictures of Terry fishing. The other desk was plastered with dozens of pictures of young, blurry-eyed female patrons.

She knew these pictures had been taken by John's uncle, Art. He was a dirty old man who loved to joke to Corrine about how he had her eighteenth birthday circled on his calendar.

Corrine walked over to the desk that appeared to be shared by John and Terry and sat down.

"So, what's this about my brother?" John asked. He leaned against his uncle's desk opposite her and folded his arms.

"He's just been acting a little weird lately." Corrine said. "Haven't you noticed?"

Making it look as if she were merely fidgeting, Corrine moved aside an ashtray and looked inside of a cup holding pencils on Terry's desk.

John cleared his throat. "No more so than normal," he said. "What exactly do you mean?"

Corrine spotted a small key, half covered by a notepad for missed calls. She glanced upward and noticed the cupboard above her had a lock that was just small enough for the key to fit in.

Corrine coughed into her fist.

"I'm sorry," she said. "Do you mind if I get some water? My throat's a bit dry."

John uncrossed his arms and stood up. "Uh, yeah, sure."

John was a bit thrown off by the request, but still didn't appear to suspect anything. "I'll be right back," he said.

Corrine smiled sweetly. As soon as the door shut behind him, she shot out of her chair and grabbed the key. The cupboard unlocked easily. She stood up on the chair to get a better look inside, but found nothing more than scrap papers and a couple of unopened packs of cigarettes.

Corrine hopped down from the chair and threw open the two small drawers on the desk.

As she was rummaging inside, the door to the office started to turn. Corrine slammed the drawers shut and quickly straightened up.

John looked around the office as he entered. He held out a pint glass filled with water.

Corrine grabbed the glass. "Thanks," she said. Taking a sip of water she walked out of the room past him and said, "You know what? It's a little hot back here; maybe we should go talk in the bar."

John looked absolutely confused. "Hot? It's like sixty degrees."

"You know us women," Corrine joked. "We can never pick a temperature."

He chuckled, encouraged by her playful response.

"You mind if I go behind the bar?" she asked.

John took a quick survey of the place. They weren't technically open yet, so he and Corrine were the only ones inside and his uncle didn't usually show up until after lunch. "I guess...."

Corrine sauntered behind the bar. "I've been looking to make some extra money," she said. "Whaddya think? I know I'm not old enough yet, but maybe I could help out. Ya know, get glasses and stuff?"

Corrine leaned suggestively over the counter. "How do I look?" she asked.

"What's this all about, Corrine?" John put his hands down on the bar in front of her and leaned in. "Do you want a job, or do you want to talk to me about my brother?"

Corrine's obvious attempts to flirt with John weren't going over as she had hoped. Deciding to switch tactics, Corrine let out a sigh and crossed her arms. "I think he stole something from me," she said. "I don't know, maybe I misplaced it, but he's been acting really weird with me and before I go accusing anyone, I guess I just wanted to check with you to see if he had a history of this kind of stuff."

John pulled out a bar stool and took a seat. "What exactly do you think he took?"

"I mean, it's nothing expensive or anything."

She feigned deep concern as she continued with, "John, you don't think Terry's doing drugs, do you?"

The question obviously shocked John. But then again, he knew his brother and he knew Terry was quite capable of really anything. "Why?"

"It's just...." Corrine stopped herself and bit her lower lip like she wasn't sure if she should say something.

"What is it, Corrine? If there's something you know, I think I have the right to know, too."

Corrine leaned in and in a hushed tone said, "He stopped me on the way to work this morning and he kind of scared me."

"Well, what did he do?" John asked.

"He was rambling on and on about some crazy stuff—and then he sorta—well he sorta grabbed me."

"He grabbed you?"

"Yeah," she said, tugging at her sleeves. "He pushed me up against a wall."

"What? You're kidding!"

John may have been a pig, but he was an old school Midwestern boy. Putting your hands on a woman was completely off limits.

Encouraged by John's response, Corrine decided to finish Terry off. "Yeah," she said. "I know. I couldn't believe it either. But what really scared me was—he asked me if I had something-"

"Good God, what?" John asked.

"I think he was asking me to give him jewelry," she said. "So he could like sell it or something? I don't know. Again, he wasn't making much sense—so I couldn't really understand him."

John leaned back in his chair. "Whoa...."

Corrine felt the control shift back to her as she walked out from behind the bar. "So anyway, I just wanted to make sure you were aware, ya know?" she said. "Just in case he starts acting funny."

John stood up as she came over to him. "Well, I'll keep my eye on him."

"One more thing—" Corrine added.

"Yeah?"

"Just in case he did steal this thing of mine. Does he have a hiding place or anything? Is there any place you could look?"

John thought about it a moment. "Well it wouldn't be here," he said. "I know where everything is."

"What about your house?" Corrine asked.

Before John could answer, the phone in his pocket started ringing. He took it out and looked at the number calling. "It's Terry," he said.

John held his finger to his lips to signal she should be quiet as he answered.

Corrine could hear Terry screaming through the receiver.

She listened to John try to quiet him. "Calm down, Terry. Okay. Just calm down. I'm sure your keys are around. Why would somebody take them? Okay. Stay there. I'll come and get you." Then John added, "I think we need to have a talk when I get there."

"What's going on?" Corrine asked when he hung up the phone.

"I think you're right."

John walked over to the coat rack by the door and put on his jacket.

"Don't worry," he said. "I'll straighten him out."

༄༅

Corrine giggled and flashed a devious smile at me. "So Terry may know we have the talisman, but John's now totally convinced he either has a bad drug problem or is a total mental case. One mention of a magic necklace and that house will be boarded up so tight, Terry'll never get out."

I slapped my knees and laughed so hard that I started choking.

Corrine laughed too, taking a corner, and turning the wheel sharply to the right. We were about five miles off of Main Street by now.

"So, where are we going?" I asked.

"To my place. I figure if Terry does get out, he'll go straight to your apartment. We should lay low tonight. He won't go to my house with my parents there. Can you stay over?"

"It doesn't matter," I said. "My parents are gonna ground me forever the next time they see me anyway, what's one more night? Will your parents let me stay over?"

"Not everyone's parents are as cool as yours, Travis."

She smiled over at me from the driver's seat.

"But I have something that's kinda like my own apartment."

"You do?"

Corrine just laughed. "You'll see," she said.

Chapter 22

Corrine had sneaked me into her childhood tree fort behind her house. She had told me to wait there for her until her parents went to sleep. Sitting in the middle of the floor with my knees drawn up, I felt like a giant.

Like the memories of childhood, the once-white fort was now cracked and graying. Faded flowers were painted together with green vines around its windows; through the largest of which, I could see the back of the house.

Corrine waved to me from her bedroom window on the second floor. I waved back and made a face about the fort. She laughed and mimed to me that her parents would be asleep soon.

As I waited, I looked at the walls around me. Photos of Corrine as a little girl were hung in wooden frames. They had yellowed over time, but even so, you could still tell how beautiful she was—even then. There was a huge map up there as well. Corrine had written all over it in pen, commenting on various landmarks she one day hoped to visit.

There was a hammer lying under the map which caught my eye. As I stared at it, I thought about what Doctor Kelly had said about destroying the talisman, ...that it was only to be used in the event something evil or unwanted gained entry into the Lucid.

I didn't know about evil—Terry was definitely unwanted—but he was gone now and I had the talisman. I would never let it out of my sight again.

As the hours passed, my eyes became heavy. But they stayed fixed on the hammer, somehow drawn to it.

My trance was only broken by the sound of a window opening. Although the clouds were blocking most of the light from the moon, I could still make out Corrine's form as she first climbed onto the roof of the porch, then down a trellis on the side of the house. She had obviously done this before.

I could hear her footsteps as she hurried across the grass to where I was. "Travis?" Corri whispered.

I looked down the hole in the floor.

She smiled up at me.

"You made that looked easy!" I whispered back.

Corrine threw up a blanket and a pillow that she had tucked under her arm and climbed up to meet me. "What? It's not like it's the first time." She laughed.

I stared blankly back at her.

"Oh my God! This is your first time sneaking out, isn't it?"

I was glad it was dark out so that she couldn't see me blush.

She brushed the dirt off her legs and sat down in front of me so that our knees were touching.

"Well, I'm glad I could be your first time." Corrine pecked me on the cheek and leaned back.

This wouldn't have been strange, had we been dreaming. I was used to her flirting with me there, but over the past couple of days I had noticed some of the same behavior creeping outside of the dreams.

"I haven't been up here in forever," she said, looking around the tree house. "Pretty cool place I have here, right?"

"I like it," I said.

She sounded so happy, so comfortable. Like she thought all of our problems were over now that Terry was out of the way.

"Corrine, listen. Remember when I said I had something I had to tell to you?" I said. "Well, I'm ready to tell you now."

"Okay." Corrine straightened up and gave me her full attention. "I'm ready. What is it?"

"I can't tell you here," I said. "I want to tell you in the dreams."

She slumped forward. "You're killin' me! We got the talisman back. Why all the suspense? What's left? I mean, I like a good surprise and all—" She stopped herself. "It is a good surprise, right?"

"It could be. I don't really know yet."

"Huh, you're really building this thing up, aren't ya? Well…what are we waiting for?" Corrine spread the blanket out on the floor. "It's been so easy for me lately," she bragged as she smoothed out the corners of the blanket. "I just close my eyes—and it's like -bam!—I'm there."

"That's great." My voice was flat. The ease of which she spoke did not lead me to believe our discussion tonight would have anything to do with her having a choice.

I had made my dream come true, all right. In the most horrible and deceitful of ways, I had assured myself an eternity with my own personal fantasy. I still didn't have to tell her, I thought. I could always continue the lie—say I didn't know we'd be trapped there together. But that would keep her a dream, wouldn't it?

When you live a lie it's the same thing as living in a dream. In the back of your mind you'll always know the reality you think you've created doesn't really exist.

My heart was heavy as I watched Corrine lie down. Her hair spread around her like a wide band of silk. As she patted the ground next to her for me to join her, I put a hand out to stop her.

"Not yet," I said. "I need you to let me do something first."

"What's that?"

"I need you to let me go first," I instructed her. "When you're absolutely sure I'm asleep, give me about an hour before you come in."

Corrine lifted herself up on her elbows. "Seriously?"

I lay down on the floor of the tree house next to her and put my arms by my sides. "There's just one more thing I have to do."

"What's going on?"

"That's what I'm going to find out."

"You said this might be a good surprise, remember?"

"That's not entirely up to me," I said. "But don't worry." I gave her a wink and then closed my eyes. "See ya in an hour."

Chapter 23

Picture frames and old musty books began to take shape all around me. I focused all of my attention on her office, screaming Doctor Kelly's name into the pale yellow walls.

I was screaming so loud that it nearly drowned out her laughter as Kelly materialized in the chair behind her desk.

"Geez, Travis, yelling like dat I'm surprised you didn't just wake me up!"

Kelly gave me a moment to catch my breath.

"Nicely done," she marveled, taking in her office. "I must say you've got quite an eye for detail."

She spun around once in her chair and then stood up to greet me. "I'm on my way back to see you, you know. Must be a smoode flight if I'm sleeping dis well," she joked.

"You're not in Holland anymore?"

"I couldn't stay one minute longer," she gushed. "I was so excited by our developments here dat I had to come back and see you."

"I let someone in," I blurted.

Kelly stopped dead in her tracks. "What did you say?"

"I let someone in."

Her face fell. Kelly had to put a hand on the corner of the desk to steady herself. "What do you mean you let someone in?" she asked. "Who?"

"It's this guy. It was this guy," I said, the words tripping over themselves. "He stole the talisman, but we got it back. We got it back and–and–and he's out now. So it's okay. Everything's okay, right? He's out now." I repeated.

Doctor Kelly brought her hand to her forehead and rubbed the space between her eyes.

"Wait a second. Back up a moment," she said. "We? Does dis mean dat dis girl has decided to stay here wid you?"

I looked down at the floor, thoroughly ashamed. Mumbling under my breath I answered, "I haven't asked her yet."

Kelly sank down on the corner of the desk. "I should have stayed," she wheezed.

The look on her face was telling me exactly what I didn't want to hear.

"But he's gone! He doesn't have the talisman anymore. Besides, it's not like anyone is ever gonna believe anything he says!"

Kelly let out a mournful sigh and put her hands on her hips. "Travis, I don't zink you fully understand what has happened here. Not only have you brought someone in widdout deir consent, but you've also allowed an outsider in. Dat dreatens da safety of our entire world! Dere's only one zing dat can be done in a situation like dis...."

She waited for me to answer.

Hesitant, I eeked out, "I have to destroy the talisman?"

"What odder option could dere be, Travis?! It needs to be done right now—da moment dat you wake up!"

"No!" I cried. "Why?! Nobody has to know—"

Her voice boomed like thunder as she got to her feet. "Stop dis! Dere are rules here, Travis! As a keeper of da talisman, you are expected to abide by zose rules. And if you break dem? You must pay da price. You were given a great gift—and you have abused dat power. You are no longer welcome here."

My eyes welled up with tears. "But—if I destroy it? Is the Lucid over? How can anyone else ever get in?"

"Please," she quipped. "What do you take me for? Do you really zink I would trust dat kind of power in da hands of a teenage boy? Not dat da talisman wasn't something very special–it was."

Kelly crossed her arms and looked down her nose at me. "Dere are odder means of accessing dis world."

"And Corrine?" I choked.

"What about her?" she said coolly. "She won't remember any interaction she's had wid you about da dreams. You will boz go back to being exactly who you were a few weeks ago–no memory, no consequences, no regret."

"Except for me," she added. "I am the only one dat will have any knowledge of dis whole terrible event."

I covered my face with my hands.

"What?" Kelly asked. "If you ask me, you all get off radder easy for what you've done."

"But I love her!" I wailed. "Corrine would never talk to me without remembering any of this. She wouldn't like me out there! She—she–I can't go back, Doctor Kelly! I can't!"

My shoulders heaved in great sobs and I couldn't catch my breath long enough to say anything else.

"Casting yourself out is da only way to cast out da odders, Travis. Dere is no choice in any of dis."

I started to bawl like a baby in front of Doctor Kelly, I couldn't help it. Saliva frothed up at the corners of my mouth like sea foam, spilling down to mix with the large round tears that rolled down my face. It was an embarrassing display for me, but for Kelly it was a reminder. I was crying like a child, because I was in fact just that: I was still a child.

Kelly grabbed a box of tissues from her desk and handed them to me.

Snatching a big handful out of the box, I blew my nose into them with a loud awkward honk.

Kelly's icy exterior started to melt as she watched me. And the next words she spoke came out with a somewhat surprising maternal quality to them. "Dat girl you say you love? She is part of us now. Do you zink it was fair dat she wasn't given a choice?"

"I didn't know if she'd say yes," I sniffled.

Kelly, who was no stranger to love and loss, came over and put her arms around me.

"Tricking someone into being wid you—forcing deir hand—is not love. I know you–I know you know better dan dat."

"She likes me here," I said as I buried my head in her shoulder. "She likes who I am here."

"Oh, Travis," Kelly said, stroking my hair. "You are no different in da dreams."

"Yes, I am."

I turned my head to the side, my tears soaking the top of her soft cotton shirt. "Here I'm all the things I'm not out there. I'm confident, I'm funny, I'm brave, I'm—"

Kelly pushed me back and lifted my chin with her finger. "You zink dat da dreams did dat?"

I couldn't see her well through my tears. The contours and colors of her face blurred together like a watercolor painting that's been lifted up before it's done drying.

Kelly laughed a gentle laugh. "Dis girl was connected wid you enough to be in your dreams from da very beginning. Why do you zink dat is?"

I shook my head. I really had no idea. If anything, I thought my draw to Corrine was enough for the both of us—enough for a hundred people.

"Dreams are nozing more dan situations your mind creates. How you react in dose situations is up to you. And dat is what da Lucid is all about—finding your true self through extraordinary circumstances."

"But all I've learned about myself is how horrible I can be!" I moaned.

"Travis, we can't learn or appreciate any of da good zings about ourselves widdout learning da bad. Dat is precisely how we learn." Kelly paused and thought about what she had said. "Huh…In dat case… I suppose… da Lucid did do what it is intended to."

She took a step back and nodded. "Granted it is not da best ending, but—still, you found yourself. Not only dat, you found each odder."

"What am I supposed to do?" I begged.

"You must destroy da talisman," Kelly said again. "Dat has not changed."

"But I told Corrine to meet me here," I said sheepishly. "She'll be falling asleep any minute."

Doctor Kelly flashed a crooked smile. "Ahh, I see. You still want to see her? Is dat it?"

It was so selfish, but I did. I did want to see her. And I didn't care if I'd never remember any of it.

"Dis hurt will go away da moment you break da stone," she said. Her voice was filled with a deep and profound compassion.

"Can I?" I whispered, begging. "Can I see her tonight?"

"If I let you-" Doctor Kelly said. "Will you promise me one zing?"

"Anything."

"Do not tell her dat it is da last night. It is better not to know dese zings. Can you do dat?"

I nodded vigorously. A wave of emotions rushed over me—sadness for Kelly, excitement for myself, and then suddenly—fear.

"What if Terry—what if the person I let in finds us?" I thought out loud.

"Mmm. I zink I can keep him away," she said. "Dis one time zough. Dis one time, and only for love."

Kelly smiled and swept her hand over my face. "Close your eyes."

"I'm sorry for what I did," I said as I shut my eyes. "I'm sorry I let all of these things happen."

"Life isn't about da mistakes we make, Travis," she whispered. It's how we move forward from dem dat is da true test of our character. Now go."

"Enjoy what little time you have left wid her."

Chapter 24

What do you say to someone you know you'll never see again? Where would you go to spend your last moments with them, if you could go anywhere? Those questions may seem difficult, or like they should have some grand solutions, but when you're actually faced with the situation, the answers are surprisingly simple.

You don't think of exotic places or of long speeches you want to deliver like the ones you see in the movies. You just say whatever you want to say and go wherever your mind takes you.

My mind took me to where I saw Corrine at her best.

And when she finally appeared in the distance, I watched with amusement as she looked down at what she was wearing and laughed. It was the same flowing white dress she had been wearing the first time we met.

I stood next to the lake, my hands clasped behind me, waiting for her where it all began.

"This is what you were doing?" she joked as she walked across the field towards me. Dandelion seeds danced and swirled around her legs and the setting sun burned behind her like fire as she moved.

I could have dreamed about this moment a thousand times, but a million dreams and a million fantasies could never have done it justice.

When Corrine reached me she asked, "So what's this important thing you have to tell me?"

"You just made me forget."

"Forget what?"

"Forget everything." I grabbed her around the waist and kissed her.

A strong breeze lifted up from the ground as I kissed her: it circled our feet, our bodies, and our hair. It seemed impossible to me that those long fiery golden locks of hers, that has so captivated me the first time I saw her, were the same ones now brushing across my face.

Corrine used one hand to pull her hair back behind her. She kept her eyes closed as she stepped away from me, smiling.

"I love you," I said. "That's all I wanted to tell you. That's all I've ever wanted to tell you."

Corrine opened her eyes slowly. "That's all?" she asked with a sly smile. "Well, I already knew that. Why else would we be doing all of this?"

She leaned forward, kissed me softly on the lips, then leaned back. She whispered, "I love you too, Travis."

They were just four tiny little words, but the weight of them together was enough to make my legs buckle. Falling to my knees, I groaned and grabbed her hips. "Why do you have to do this to me?" I pleaded, barely able to form the words. "Why now?"

I pressed my head to her stomach and rolled my head back and forth. "Why couldn't we have met before? Why couldn't you have loved me before all of this?"

Corrine got down on her knees with me. "I didn't know you before." She took my hands and kissed them.

I grabbed her hands back. Turning them over in my own, I studied each delicate finger as I asked the question that only I knew the real answer to, "What happens now?"

Corrine brought her face closer to mine. "Well, I guess we do what normal boyfriends and girlfriends do," she said. "I hear people do that, you know? Have boyfriends and girlfriends?"

I winced. Her playful caricature of me cut into my heart like a knife. I needed to ground myself—to remind myself that this wasn't all real.

"You mean in the dreams, right?" I asked. "You mean we'll be a couple in the dreams?"

Corrine cocked her head to the side. "Travis, we've spent most of our time outside of the dreams, haven't we? I'm your girlfriend here. And I'm your girlfriend there."

I couldn't process what she was saying. "But what about how I look?"

"What about it?"

"I don't look like this out there."

"You don't look like what?"

"Like this," I ran my hands down in front of my body. "Doctor Kelly told me that you see what you want to see in the dreams—what you desire. That's why you see me like this."

Corrine shook her head, obviously confused. "Travis, what are you talking about?"

"Do I have to spell it out for you? I'm handsome in the dreams. That's why you want to be with me," I said. "Because I look the way you want me to look here."

Corrine snapped back, stunned, like she had just been slapped in the face. "Yes, you are what I want you to look like in the dreams. But you look exactly the same way you do-" She stopped. "Wait? You mean you think—"

Corrine cast her eyes downward at the lake as she put it all together. A butterfly sent ripples across the surface of the water and Corrine's face immediately brightened. "Look!" She grabbed me by the arm and dragged my body toward the lake's edge.

She pulled me down so that we were kneeling side by side and pushed my face toward the water. I tried to push back, but she kept insisting. When I finally looked down I saw what Corrine was trying to tell me. There was no denying the image. There shining brightly back at me from the water's surface was a crystal clear reflection of my real self.

I felt my breath escape me. "But—I don't understand," I stammered. "When we first met, you didn't recognize me. What about the junkyard? In the ballroom?"

She looked in the water with me so that her reflection was now shining next to mine.

"You're right," she said. "I didn't see you like this at first. I don't know why I didn't. But ever since we really met? Since I found out who you really were?" Corrine's reflection in the water turned toward mine. "I've seen you just like this, Travis. And that's who I want to see. That's who I love."

"But I saw myself in the mirrors," I protested, unconvinced. "I saw myself in the ballroom. I didn't look like this."

"You said Doctor Kelly told you we get to see the things we want to see in the dreams, right? Well if that's true—seeing you like that wasn't my desire," she said. "It must have been yours."

I looked up from the water at Corrine. She smiled, nodding at me with wide eyes, happy with herself for solving the puzzle. A desperate groan escaped from the depths of my soul as what she was saying registered. I rocked sideways into her and covered my face with my hands, my shoulders shaking with great silent sobs.

Corrine moved her arms around me and held me. "There's no reason to be so upset," she said. "None of that stuff matters now. We found each other, right? We have all the time in the world to make up for anything else."

I dug my fingers into my legs and breathed in deep through my nose to steel myself. Summoning all of the courage and strength that I had, I pushed myself back to face her.

"You're killing me," I said in a low voice. I cleared my throat to try to keep it from cracking. "You're absolutely killing me right now."

Perplexed, Corrine furrowed her brow. Not knowing what to do, she diffused the situation in the way that only she could. "This is getting waayyy too heavy, isn't it?"

Corrine got to her feet and smoothed out her dress with her hands. "This is our first official date, Travis. And I hate to tell you this, but you're really kinda blowin it right now."

I didn't know what to say.

She smiled and put her hands on her hips. "Well, come on. You know, if you're going to be a good boyfriend, you really have to start getting used to the idea that us girlfriends usually get our way."

My smile felt more like a wince as I looked up at her.

She grabbed my arm and pulled me to my feet, like a begrudging old man. "There. That's more like it!"

Corrine put an arm on my shoulder for support as she kicked off her shoes. "Let's go swimming."

"I can't swim." I sighed.

"Ahhh," Corrine breathed, circling me. "You can do anything here. Didn't you tell me that?"

"I did," I said, nodding. "You're absolutely right. You can do anything here."

With that, she slapped my arm, just like the first time, and took off running toward the water.

The difference this time? I didn't hesitate. I didn't fight the moment. I went with it with everything I had.

She laughed relentlessly, the water splashing up all around us, and I came bounding in the water after her.

It was my first date with the woman I loved, who loved me back, and although neither of us would ever remember it, I'd be damned if I was going to ruin it.

After we went swimming, I asked her to sit in the grass with me like we had before.

I lay with my head in her lap, staring up at the sky as we talked and laughed about all of the moments which had gotten us to this point. It was the most perfect first date that ever was.

"If you thought it was okay for us to change our appearances, I'm surprised you didn't give me bigger boobs," she joked.

I laughed and stuck a blade of grass in between my teeth. "I thought about it."

She slapped me playfully on the arm.

"Why do you think we're here, anyway?" I asked. "How do you think we ended up in the dreams together?"

"I've been thinking about that a lot lately."

"You have?"

"Mmm. Hmm." Corrine leaned back on her hands. "You know, I noticed you before, at the coffee shop."

I rolled my eyes up at her in surprise.

"I did," she said. "You were so quiet, but you seemed okay with it—like you had a secret world in your head that nobody knew about. I wondered what it would feel like to be so comfortable in your own skin like that. Not to feel like you had to act like someone else all the time."

"You thought I was comfortable in my own skin?" I laughed.

"I think you were right," she said. "At the coffee shop? When you said we shared the same dream."

"How's that?"

"Dreams aren't just when you're sleeping, are they? They're part of that gray space, where your mind goes when it wanders—the things we don't say—the feelings and fantasies we keep to ourselves, they're the spaces between the lines of the story. That's the place where dreams are born, and I think that's where we connect."

"What the . . . hell?" I jumped up off her lap and turned around to face her. "Corrine, don't take this the wrong way, but your looks are nothing— I mean, nothing— compared to your mind."

"Travis Hunter, I do believe that's the nicest back-handed compliment, I've ever received."

She leaned forward and kissed me. We had kissed a number of times in this dream, but it was fresh and exciting each time. I could kiss her for hours. Days. Years.

But unfortunately our time was running out.

"I feel myself getting lighter," she said as she pulled back. "We'll be waking up soon."

She was right. We had gotten used to that kind of numb, tingly feeling. From previous experience, we knew that when this happened it was only a matter of time, maybe ten minutes or less, before the dream ended.

"I have one more surprise for you," I whispered.

"Another one?" Corrine giggled. "Honestly, I don't know how many more of these I can take."

"This'll be the last one for a while, I promise. But I need your help to do it."

"What is it?"

"I have something to give you—out of the dream, that is. I need you to let me wake myself up first."

"I guess I can do that." She smiled. "You better hurry, though. I don't know how much longer I can stay asleep."

"No problem."

I stared at her trying to soak in every last detail. "Thank you." I said.

"For what?"

"For making me comfortable in my own skin."

"Me, too." Corrine gave me one more quick peck. "Now you better hurry up or I'm gonna wake up and ruin your surprise if ya don't. Oh! And whatever you plan on doing, be quiet, I don't want you to wake my parents up."

"You got it."

I was afraid if I held this out any longer, I would lose my nerve and she deserved so much more than what I had done to her.

"I'll see you soon," I said, and closed my eyes.

I wanted it to be true. I wanted it to be true with every fiber of my being. The last thing I saw before I woke up was her smiling back at me.

ಲಿಬ

Dawn was just beginning to break as I grabbed the hammer from the floor of the tree house. I couldn't bring myself to look at her, only pausing briefly at the bottom of the ladder.

I pulled the talisman from my pocket and made a wish to whatever powers connected me with the stone. "Let her remember me," I whispered. "Please. I'll do anything. Just let her remember me." Then looking up towards where she slept, I added, "I love you Corrine," and took off running.

Chapter 25

"Corrine? Mrs. Johnson? It's nice to meet you boz. Come on in." Mrs. Johnson pumped the pretty doctor's hand up and down. "Oh, I'm so happy to meet you! You come highly recommended. I can't believe you were able to see my daughter so quickly. Everyone else was booked a month out!"

"Well, I just got back from a vacation so my schedule was wide open. Please, take a seat." Doctor Kelly sat down as well and opened a folder in front of her at her desk.

"I have here dat you're having trouble sleeping, Corrine? Is dat right?"

Mrs. Johnson immediately answered for her daughter. "It's the weirdest thing. Corrine just woke up in her tree house the other night. Can you imagine? Sleepwalking outside? What if she was hit by a car?"

"Is dis true, Corrine?"

Corrine looked up at the doctor. "Yes," she said quietly.

"Tell her the other thing, dear," her mother prompted.

Corrine looked uncomfortable, "I've forgotten some things too," she said. "Like I can't remember what I did some nights."

Mrs. Johnson jumped in again. "I mean at first I thought drugs, you know? She's a kid and all, but she swears that's not the case. Of course I'd take drugs over any kind —any kind of—" Mrs. Johnson leaned in and whispered loudly, "any kind of mental illness." She flew back in her chair, her hand to her chest. "Oh please, just tell us it's not that. This is normal, right? There's some kind of medication you can give her, right?"

Doctor Kelly continued to write. "I'm not dat kind of doctor," she said. "But I see here dat you're going to be a senior dis year. Dat's a very stressful time in a young woman's life. Sleep problems are often associated wid stress."

There was a loud knock on the door frame and all three of them looked up. It was the woman from the front desk. "Doctor Kelly? Your other patient is here."

"Ah! Great." Kelly said. "Send him in, please."

She closed the file she was working on and stood up.

"Dere's someone else I want you to meet."

Corrine recognized the boy in the hallway immediately. He was the strange-looking boy who came to her store all the time. He hadn't been by lately and she didn't know why, but for some reason it made her happy to see him standing there.

"Come on in," Kelly beckoned to the boy.

He looked nervously at the two chairs. "There's nowhere to sit," he mumbled.

Corrine looked at the boy. His hands were shoved deep in his pockets. Corrine thought he looked just as uneasy as she felt.

"Actually, Mrs. Johnson? Would you mind if dese two talked wid me?" Kelly asked. "Alone?"

Corrine's mother looked quite surprised.

When she failed to move, Kelly tried again. "Would you mind waiting in da lobby, Mrs. Johnson?"

"Wh—Why would I do that?"

"I zink dese two have quite a bit in common."

Mrs. Johnson looked thoroughly revolted by the notion.

"What on earth could these two have in common?" she snorted.

Doctor Kelly cleared her throat. "Well, for one, dey are boz da same age, but more importantly dey have boz had parents call me dis week about similar kinds of stress-related sleeping problems."

Mrs. Johnson looked unconvinced. "Isn't this rather unorthodox?"

"Wid kids dis age, group therapy wid peers is often da most powerful solution." Doctor Kelly leaned in and in a hushed tone added, "It could save you from a lot of problems down the road—if you know what I mean."

Mrs. Johnson looked over at Corrine as she got up from her seat. "Well, I don't know..."

"It's quite normal to be apprehensive about zerapy, but just give it a try," Kelly pushed. "Ask Corrine how she feels about it and if da sleep problems aren't coming back, I'd continue wid dis for a while."

"You would?" Mrs. Johnson said.

"I would."

"Well, you're the expert," Mrs. Johnson conceded. Before walking out to the lobby she called back to Corrine. "I'll be right out here, honey," Then motioning to the young man, "...you know, if you need me."

Corrine hung her head, mortified by her mother's behavior as the boy took a seat next to her.

Doctor Kelly shut the door.

"Ok, you two," she said. "We're going to do somezing kids your age don't normally do."

The two teens looked up at her, utterly confused, as she took a seat on the edge of her desk.

"We're going to talk. Not on da web, not on da phone, I mean we're going to talk, face to face, zree strangers, getting to know each odder. Maybe you've read about dis in your history books, but dat's how us old folks used to communicate."

Corrine chuckled, which made the boy next to her smile, although he tried to hide it.

"Now I know dat everyone wants a quick fix to deir problems," Kelly continued. "Dey just want a pill, or a game, or to wave some magic wand dat will solve all of deir problems." Kelly folded her hands in front of her. "But we as human beings can offer each odder far more dan any computers, pills, or magic ever could. In fact we can offer each odder somezing more powerful dan all of zose zings combined. We just have to get to know one anodder to find out what it is."

Doctor Kelly looked at the two teens, who were now both staring awkwardly at the floor.

"So let's get started," she said.

"Travis—dis is Corrine. Corrine—dis is Travis."

About the author

Natalie Roers is a veteran writer, voice artist, and on-air personality. A journalist by trade, Lucid is her first work of fiction. She is busy at work on her second novel and hopes to raise money and social awareness for worthy causes with each book she writes. Natalie plans to donate a portion of every sale of this book to her favorite anti-bullying organizations. She lives with her husband Cory, and son Austin, in Columbia, South Carolina.

Don't miss any of these
other exciting SF/F books

➤ *Angelos*
(1-933353-60-0, $16.95 US)

➤ *Gaea*
(1-60619-183-7, $18.95)

➤ *Griffin Rising* - Book 1
(1-60619-210-8, $15.95 US)

➤ *Griffin's Fire* - Book 2
(1-60619-212-4, $15.95 US)

➤ *Shadows of Kings*
(1-60619-223-x, $17.95 US)

➤ *The Coal Elf*
(1-60619-216-7, $16.95 US)

➤ *The Nameless Prince*
(1-60619-243-6, $16.95 US)

Twilight Times Books
Kingsport, Tennessee

Order Form

If not available from your local bookstore or favorite online bookstore, send this coupon and a check or money order for the retail price plus $3.50 s&h to Twilight Times Books, Dept. LS713 POB 3340 Kingsport TN 37664. Delivery may take up to two weeks.

Name: _____

Address: _____
_____

Email: _____

I have enclosed a check or money order in the amount of

$_____

for _____ .

If you enjoyed this book, please post a review
at your favorite online bookstore.

Twilight Times Books
P O Box 3340
Kingsport, TN 37664
Phone/Fax: 423-323-0183
www.twilighttimesbooks.com/

CPSIA information can be obtained at www.ICGtesting.com
Printed in the USA
LVOW10s1009200713

343854LV00001B/202/P